OH, TO BE
MONSTROUS

HAZEL HYDE

MILTON & HUGO L.L.C.
1001 3rd Avenue West, Suite 430
Bradenton, FL 34205, USA

Website: *www. miltonandhugo.com*
Hotline: *1- 888-778-0033*
Email: *info@miltonandhugo.com*

Ordering Information:
Quantity sales. Special discounts are granted to corporations, associations, and other organizations. For more information on these discounts, please reach out to the publisher using the contact information provided above.

ISBN-13:   979-8-89285-787-1   [Paperback Edition]
             979-8-89285-786-4   [Digital Edition]

Rev. date: 02/13/2026

INTRODUCTION

Three quotes, three separate times, have inspired me to either put this book to paper or to return to this book after much time.. Three quotes resonated with me with words I've never been able to vocalize. These are those quotes.

"I always had a repulsive need to be something more than human."

—David Bowie

"'You're not a monster,' I said. But I lied. What I really wanted to say was that a monster is not such a terrible thing to be. From the Latin root monstrum, a divine messenger of catastrophe, then adapted by the Old French to mean an animal of myriad origins: centaur, griffin, satyr. To be a monster is to be a hybrid signal, a lighthouse: both shelter and warning at once."

—Ocean Vuong

"I will say this as bluntly as I know how: I am a transsexual, and therefore I am a monster. Just as the words "dyke", "fag", "queer", "slut", and "whore" have been reclaimed, respectively, by lesbians and gay men, by anti assimilationist sexual minorities, by women who pursue erotic pleasure, and by sex industry workers, words like "creature", "monster", and "unnatural" need to be reclaimed by the transgendered. [...] Hearken unto me, fellow creatures. I who have dwelt in a form unmatched with my desire, I whose flesh has become an assemblage of incongruous anatomical parts, I who achieve the similitude of a natural body only through an unnatural process, I offer you this warning: the Nature you bedevil me with is a lie. Do not trust it to protect you from what I represent, for it is a fabrication that cloaks the groundlessness of the privilege you seek to maintain for yourself at my expense. You are as constructed as me; the same anarchic womb has birthed us both. I call upon you to investigate your nature as I have been compelled to confront mine. I challenge you to risk abjection and flourish as well as have I. Heed my words, and you may well discover the seams and sutures in yourself."

—Susan Stryker

For all those who always loved the monsters and never themselves.

Chapter 1

THE RITUAL

My name is Daxton Meyers, but it won't be for long. Soon I will be nothing more than a whisper on the wind and a shadow in the night. I'll be nothing but an urban legend, talked about at sleepovers and by cryptid fanatics. That, or I will have failed, and won't be anything at all.

I am not, and never have been, a boy. I've never been human in the first place either.

Inside me has always been this aching hunger. This monstrous appetite. Gnashing teeth, sharp claws, and jagged spines all tear at my flesh under the surface. All urging to become. I've never been just another human as I have always been a Monster. Something great and terrible. Something capable and untouchable. Something more.

Yet, here I am. I pretend to smile and laugh with other kids at school in futile attempts to not be ostracized. I have pale skin, black wavy hair, and disgustingly regular brown eyes. I even have a pet dog, Rascal. I'm average. I'm far from normal, as is clear to anyone who spends extended time with me, but I have the world convinced I'm both human and a boy and thus am trapped by humanity and manhood both.

I have to maintain this ruse for fear of... well, what people do to monsters, freaks, and those they just don't understand. I have to maintain this secret for a while longer though. No one would ever understand what it means for me to become on the outside what I am on the inside. Soon though, people will finally know me. I won't have to pretend and lie. I won't feel hollow when I laugh or have to force myself to smile day after day. I will truly, finally be myself with every fiber of my being.

I've always had a fascination with the occult. An obsession really. The possibility of power lying hidden in dead languages gave way to the hope of transformation. Hope of Change. I've scoured every book in the library on magic throughout history and cultures and tried every spell on every blog I've seen to find any trace of something I could use. Nothing. Nothing has provided me with any real help. Any real power.

Finally, however, I have something new. Something older. Rumors around town whisper of an abandoned shack no one goes near, deep in the woods. A spot where some Satanists tried to summon the antichrist. Where the ghosts of those get lost in the woods dwell. Where every boogeyman and local cryptid lives supposedly. There lies as good a chance as any at something fantastical.

No one goes near it. Mostly because barely anyone thinks it's real, let alone talks about it. It is real though. My only true friend, Alex, told me exactly how to find it.

It's impossible to get to without spending at least one night in the woods. These woods are known to have bears in them so no one besides me or Alex would risk it. Having ran away from home many times, even running into each other in these woods, means Alex was able to discover the shack with enough time and luck.

I however did what Alex couldn't. I've picked the lock and found my way inside. Among the dusty shelves and cobwebs, I found a few things: an old busted rifle, some expired food, a torn family photo showing no faces, and a number of books. Among them, a singular journal, bound shut with red twine. When I broke the red seal with my knife and opened the journal, the temperature dropped several degrees from a small chill in the night air to making me shiver.

I knew I had found what I've been looking for. It took me another day or so in these woods to make it home. My folks had barely recognized my absence.

"Go shower, you smell like shit," is my welcome home. My mother's interpretation of a warm welcome. Almost eighteen years of close proximity hasn't resulted in any level of closeness. My father passed out on the couch again, drunk as usual if the empty glasses on the coffee table were any indicator.

I go downstairs to the unfinished basement, ignoring my mother's demands and drag my tired and aching body directly to my room. I ignore the growling of my stomach as well. I forgot to pack food for the way back. Or rather I didn't expect to come back if I'm being honest with myself, but the contents of the journal were... unclear. Diagrams and pictures, every other page displaying sigils and body parts and what must be demons. To top it all off, all of the writing in a language I can't recognize.

It takes me the rest of the day, scouring the internet to figure out what language it's in. It's seven. Seven separate languages, all used interchangeably as if the writer spoke them all fluently or it was written by many people at once.

From Latin to modern day German and Spanish. It took me a week to be able to understand the basics. I quickly thank Google Translate and the internet in general.

Whoever wrote the journal and for what purpose remain a mystery. It's not a list of rituals like I first suspected either. It's all the different components and parts needed to make a ritual from scratch. Demons to commune with, comparing values of sacrificial materials, lists of things that correspond to other things, and more. Like puzzle pieces with no actual picture goal. But I already have a goal. Become a Monster.

It takes me a few days to get what I need. I skip school and avoid my parents where I can for the time being. I already had gemstones and plants from failed spell attempts in the past. I grab everything that appears in this book corresponding to change, transformation, and rebirth: Pomegranate seeds, moonstone, peridot. Hardest of all to get, some monkshood, tied to many stories of monsters. Poisonous but not illegal to own.

I handle all these things with care, as if every one of them is full of toxins instead of the one. I grind the ingredients up and mix them together at home. I spend my time in class doodling sigils from memory. I recite the name of the demon I've chosen to fulfill my goals as I go to sleep like it's a prayer: Domina Mutationis, The Lady of Change, Bringer of Both Great and Terrible, Teratranza.

The night I'm finally ready for my homemade ritual is a quiet one. Dad's TV drones upstairs and mom has gone to bed early to pick up another shift. I lock Rascal out of my room. I don't want him to be collateral. I arrange some candles and turn off the lights. Lighting them one by one as I recite Teratranza's name and titles. I speak the best Latin I can.

"Mutatio Domina, edax veterum. convivium tibi offero." Lady of Change, consumer of the old. I offer you a feast. It is as the last candle is lit, I reach for my knife among the arrangements I've made. I cut my palm as quickly as I can. It is intense but not the worst I've experienced. I don't have time to enjoy the sight of my own blood in the candlelight as I normally would. My morbid fascination with blood has always been a subject to hide.

As soon as the small bowl with the mixture of materials begins to overflow with my blood, something changes. The concrete turns black around where the blood touches. Although it is both dim and I am lightheaded, the inky pool of darkness spreads to the circle of candles with certainty. No hallucination nor illusion. The ground is black and full of stars. I feel as if I'm floating. Excitement roars in my ears. This is it! This is-

"A feast thou sayeth?" A voice cuts through the eerie silence and the crackle of small flames. It resonates from the base of my skull. The language isn't English but I understand it. I cannot see the origin. "Well? Pray tell, what it is thou hast to offer? Pray tell, what it is thou seeketh?" The voice is melodic and yet utterly cold.

"Myself." I muster through the sudden disorientation. Is the entire room space-like now?

"Oh? Well then, choose wisely young... thing. Dost thou offer thyself to me, or dost thou wish me to change thee for a price? I can tell this is not thy true form, oh, pitiful thing." The thrumming voice fills the void I find myself in now. Her questions are followed by sudden harsh laughter like crashing cymbals.

Pitiful. That's what she sees looking at me as I am. It's the truth. I am caged. Shackled. The rest is a lie though. It's a trick. I register that much. Offer yourself and she will consume your body, leaving the ghost of your soul behind. Demand change for your body and she will consume your soul, leaving you a mindless husk of yourself. It's all in the journal. Demons never give without taking.

It took me forever to figure out the solution. That's not in the journal. I've studied mythology a lot since looking into spells and folklore. In Norse mythology, Odin sacrificed himself. He sacrificed himself to himself upon the world tree, to gain knowledge. I word this next part as carefully as I can. Practiced and repeated to myself a hundred times over by now.

"You consume the old and ancient. You bring forth the new and lustrous, but not without cost. I do not offer myself for any greater good. I do not sacrifice all that is for myself. I sacrifice myself and all that I am now so that what I truly am may be born. Consume me, and make me a Monster the likes of which I can only dream of!" I'm shouting now. My voice steadily rose as I began my speech. I doubt anything beyond this all encompassing void can hear me. The laughing falters and dies. A buzzing energy fills the air, like electricity about to arc. A mouth appears in front of me. Not a face, or an eye, or a person, but a mouth appears in the emptiness. All teeth and gum, no lips. The teeth look as sharp as daggers and are each about the size of my forearm. It slowly begins to open as in the base of my skull I hear, "Oh, thou wilt truly be fun!" I float forward without any control. The mouth seems to grow as it gets closer and closer. It opens wider and wider until it could encompass me entirely and still it continues to open. I land on a wet slathering tongue. It's... almost soft?

The jaws slam shut and instantly the pain is immense. Fire spreads up what remains of my legs. I can't see them in the darkness of this maw but I can feel the blood leaving me. The jaws open again, briefly. I glance at my floating foot and calf as the tongue pushes me around and the teeth slam down on my waist. Again, the pain is overwhelming. Agony I didn't know I could experience. Why am I not passing out? Why am I getting torn apart? Did I do something wrong? I know I said consume me but—

I am shoved against what would be cheek inside the space and turned around. The jaws open once more, my head falls and lies directly between the teeth. Panic chatters my teeth and my blood runs cold.

I am bitten and chewed to pieces. I am still awake in pieces. Some of me is floating, and some of me is caked onto pearly sharp fangs. I am barely aware of anything but the pain that fills my existence. As this is my existence now. I watch from my one intact eye as the chewing stops. The mouth opens and tongue reaches out much further than any human tongue could, gathering my floating remains. I am dragged into the mouth as Teratranza's voice permeates everything around us.

"Voracious being, pitiful flesh, all that is unsatisfied: Crave, for it is all thou knows. When did ecstasy become thy only aspiration? A ravenous consumption taking bites out of thy reason. Teeth unladen, jaws unburdened, for a divine and bloody compulsion. That exaltation found solely in the mania that is hunger. Devour, oh child, devour the bloody, the bleeding, the dying. Consume everything thou art, and hunger still."

I finally lose consciousness as I feel all over, the sensation of being swallowed.

I wake up on the floor, with a wicked headache. I feel like Zeus getting his head split open. Only instead of creating a goddess, all that comes out of me is vomit. It pools on the concrete next to the empty bowl and burnt down candles. Why is the bowl empty? Light shines through the small two foot wide window into the basement. It makes my eyes want to crawl out of my head. The start of a migraine it is then. I look around at the scene. The journal is open, the bowl empty, the candles burnt away, and vomit covers the floor.

I go and grab a rag from the laundry room, which is also in the basement, to go clean up the puke. As I'm cleaning it up, cursing myself for another failed spell and my weird ass dreams, I notice my palm. A scar runs across it, fully healed. I cut my hand. I cut my hand and it's healed?

The realization finally hits me. Something happened. I made a deal. I've done it! I did... something? Did it work? Will I finally be everything I was meant to? I take inventory of myself. I check my nails for dangerous claws. Nothing. I rush to the bathroom upstairs to look in the mirror. No shark-like teeth. Not even fangs. Nothing to speak of at all actually. Did I fuck up? Did I do something wrong? She seemed receptive to my speech? I gave that demon my blood, my body, my everything. Where is-

A sudden, gnawing pain drags me to my knees. I hit my chin on the bathroom counter on the way down, breaking skin. My hands and arms shoot to my stomach. What they are met with is not flesh. It's hard under my shirt and moving as well. Feeling clammy and faint, I quickly lift my shirt.

It's the most glorious sight I've ever seen in my life. Right above where my stomach should be located in my

8

body, from the bottom of my ribs to where my belly button should be, are sharp interlocking bones. It isn't until they shift that I realize they're teeth. A mouth with flesh torn away to reveal teeth splits open across my abdomen. It's the same mouth that devoured me last night in the void. Where organs should pour out as the jaws open, they do not. Instead, a long sharp tongue unfurls from an empty blackness inside me and licks along the jagged rows. I feel it. Fucking hell, do I start to feel it all. I feel the tongue dragging across the teeth like it's the mouth on my face. This is it. My hunger made manifest. My very desire unfolded in front of me.

"Isn't it glorious?" Asks the mouth in a humming, melodic voice I am now growing familiar with. It moves on its own, as if it were not squarely attached to my body. "Ambitious thing, tell me how thou loves what I hast done with thy body." The demon, Teratranza, questions me.

"Love doesn't even begin to describe it." I muster calmly though the excitement that has my hands shaking. A chuckle comes from the gaping hole in my body.

"Excellent." She growls. "While it is of thine own body, I will communicate through this Maw. Know that it is hungry. Know that I am hungry."

"Heh, damn. I guess I wasn't enough of a feast for you, huh? This isn't the full metamorphosis I was looking for either, but it's a good start."

"Oh, do not misunderstand, thou were positively delicious, and thy pain? Decadence. However, it is as thou hast just stated. 'It is a good start'. Thou hast successfully formed a deal with me. A contract. A covenant. Thou hast been remade with a connection to myself. Thou now hast the potential to change thyself, to manifest thy soul through thy form. Feed the both of us and thou shalt grow.

Change. I now know of the hunger that dwells within thou, and I know thou shalt know what to do. Know, however, two points, Ambitious thing. One: My hunger vastly outweighs thy own, and two: I am not known for my patience."

Another fit of crashing laughter that devolves into gnashing teeth hits my ears. Feed us? What do I feed us? I know what to feed her, but all she's I know that she eats is... oh.

I do know what she wants. The Maw quivers with anticipation as I recall being her meal. Only as I recall it, I taste it too. The blood. The flesh. That hollow empty feeling being ever so briefly full. I... was in fact delicious. My god, was I... is that what people taste like? I can't seriously be considering... I begin to salivate at the thought.

Oh. Yeah.

I'm considering it. Fuck, I'm actually considering feeding this thing people. I look at it in the mirror. As I stare at the bared fangs, I could almost close my eyes and ignore the giant mouth in my stomach if it wasn't for the small gentle movements the Maw makes at rest. I don't wish to ignore it though. As I stare at the even rows of sharp canine-like teeth, I feel warmth. I feel butterflies in my stomach and I catch myself smiling like an idiot in the mirror. A genuine, real smile for once in my life.

I'm ripped from my thoughts as I hear a pounding on the door, smile gone in an instant. "Daxton? Hurry the fuck up, I need to shower before work and you're gonna be late for school." The grouchy voice of my father makes its way to me unimpeded by the door.

"Coming!" I reply in a hurry, not wanting to anger him so early in the morning. I look back at myself in the mirror and see myself one last time. The maw seems to have stopped moving on its own. I flex it open then closed. I move its- my tongue around in my Maw. Drag it across the teeth. I feel hungry. I feel good. I drop my shirt, covering the mutation and my secret along with it. I look perfectly, disgustingly human.

For now.

Chapter 2

SCHOOL

I toss on a simple baggy black band hoodie to hide any movement of the Maw, and some black torn up jeans. While my father is showering, I quickly gargle some water from the kitchen sink to get the taste of vomit from my mouth. The imaginary taste of blood still lingers so I grab a bagel on my way out the door. Actual food seems to help with the phantom taste, though I miss the sensation as it fades.

I feel good today. I'm tired, my head is pounding, and my hair is a mess, but I feel genuinely better than I have in a long time. The walk to school feels longer than normal, which I don't mind as it gives me more time alone. I usually prefer to be alone unless it's spending time with Alex. Alex is the exception to most of my rules and boundaries.

Stuck with my thoughts and curiosity, I keep opening and closing the Maw. Feeling it as a part of me. If I open it more than a few inches, my upper torso starts to lean back. My giddiness is immense in spite of the fear of being found out. It feels so affirming to have this change, but I know the second someone finds out, they would see me as a freak, or even the monster I am. People do horrible things to the freaks. No, no one can find out until

I am unrecognizable. Untouchable. Until I pass as a true monster.

I quickly lose myself to thoughts of teeth and other possible changes, and find myself in the middle of my school's hallways, running right into the last person I wanted to see. Literally.

"Hey! Creepy ass wimps like you better watch where the fuck they're going!" Justin swiftly puts me in a headlock. He's got a solid foot on me so he does this easily. We may be in the middle of school but no one intervenes. Not a teacher in sight as usual. Justin has a way of getting away with anything, even with all these witnesses. Even if people did notice, the second they see it was me, none of them would care. His arm tightens around my throat as he yanks me around. My hands try and pry his arms free unsuccessfully. He's much stronger than me.

"What do you want, dickweed?" I sputter through choked breath. I feel strangely bold compared to my usual reserved self. I feel like I could take whatever he has to throw at me when I very clearly can't. The Maw begins to stir under my shirt, baring its fangs like a wolf.

"What was that you just said?! I'll kick your-" But he's cut off as a light in the dark shows up: Justin's twin sister, Amanda. One of two people who consider me a friend.

"What do you THINK you're doing!? I told the both of you to stop fighting." She scolds us both, despite it Justin being the one at fault.

Amanda has had to put Justin in his place many times before, so it isn't a surprise when he lets me go almost instantly.

"Now run along Justin, and get to class. Daxton and I have notes to discuss for German." Amanda orders. Justin huffs and shoots a withering glare at me. I surprise myself by matching it back.

I suddenly feel hungry. Really hungry. My gaze wavers as I realize the Maw is opening. I force it closed. I know the demon's not patient but come on, not in front of everyone. Justin takes me losing the staring match as a small victory.

"That's what I thought." He mutters to himself as he walks off, uniting with some of his friends who are also on our school's baseball team along with Justin. They were watching the incident in case he needed any help, unbothered by the fact that I have never once been able to take Justin in a fight.

You'd think that being so good at something you enjoy to the point of possibly making a career out of it would make someone more easy going or at least happier. Instead he runs around like he has to prove something to everyone he meets and be a terrorizing bully to everyone in the process. Physical size and strength are all he has on me. It's been enough to keep me in my place in his eyes though.

"Until now." Says the Maw with Teratranza's voice. She responded as if she could hear my thoughts. which for all I knew, she could.

"What was that?" Amanda asks. She looks at me with an innocent and curious expression. Her blond hair held back with a blue headband. Her white and blue porcelain styled dress falls on her body in a way that made me feel ashamed to have my body at all. How can people so effortlessly be themselves? So easily dress and present in a more feminine manner? It fills me with envy. I do my best to recover quickly and answer her question.

"Uh, I said 'It's time now.' Time to go to class, I mean. We can get there a little early and go over the homework together?" It comes out a little flustered, but Amanda is used to flustering people with her looks, so she doesn't seem suspicious of my behavior. She just grins and rolls her eyes.

"Sure, but don't go getting any ideas now, I just owe you from last time is all," she says in a way that makes it obvious that she's the one getting ideas, "You need all the help you can get for that test today, after all."

"Actually, I'll have you know I've picked up some German reading recreationally. I may have, uh, skipped the homework, but I'll ace this test!" I force a guilty smile onto my face. Smiling is always so much work, but for Amanda to consider me a friend and protect me from Justin, I have to be nice. Civil. Human.

"Ugh, fine! You can copy my answers, Mr. Confident. Let's get there before the teacher does." Amanda leads on. The Maw emits a low growl that the noise of the hallway seems to cover. I stay a few paces back behind Amanda as I follow. I start whispering to myself, hoping Teratranza can hear me.

"You can't just keep making noise and reveal me like that. This is a secret." A message not only to Teratanza, but to the Maw as well. The thing linking us together. An extension of us both. Seemingly its own entity, but reacting as I would if I didn't have to hide.

"Oh, but darling, that boy would make such good prey, would he not? A tiny mutt nipping at a wolf. Then again, there is the matter of that girl..." I can feel my torso move and shift slightly as the Maw whispers her words to me.

"There is no matter. She thinks of me as a friend. I won't hurt her. People close to me will draw attention." I answer. I don't have a good rebuttal for Justin though. Beyond the fact that Amanda might be affected by his death, I feel almost nothing for him, not even hate. I simply envy him. Envy for his strength, his muscles, and his confidence. All the things that make him untouchable, that make him thrive as he is: In the body he was born with.

His death would probably not even affect me either. Though how I'd go about it is another story. I wonder if Teratranza can see how much bigger he is than me. Can she see anything around me? She knew about the twins, but that could just be auditory.

"Oh, but the way thou'st skin doth crawl as she calls thou 'Mister' and sees thou as another boy like any other. Oh, Ambitious thing, tis not affection that drives that feeling, clearly, but... well, a sickness thou art working to rectify. A misalignment of the body and soul. Soon, thou must decide who shall fuel thy change. Choose quickly, before I make the decision for thee."

"Don't bring that up." I don't enjoy thinking about my current body. The Maw is one of the very few things about it I can actually stand let alone be content with. I don't know what to make of the second part. Just how impatient is she?

"Don't bring what up?" Says a voice behind me. Alex tosses their arms around me from behind, sneaky as ever. I jump almost a foot in the air. I turn around in their arms to see Alex smiling like an idiot as usual.

Long dark hair flows down past their shoulders and their bronze skin practically glows. Spikes and chains line their body. They're so pointy, yet give such soft hugs. Their lip ring accentuates their wicked grin. I do a quick count of their piercings as I take them in. Lip, both ears, septum, bridge and a new eyebrow piercing? Nice.

"Who are you talking to?" They ask, arms still around me as they look around. By this point we're right outside of the classroom and Amanda's already inside chatting with some of her real friends.

I have to pull back slightly, so my face isn't buried in their chest but more so that the Maw isn't pressed against them. Alex will be a danger to my secret. The one person I've established can be physically affectionate with me. We both grew up as outcasts for our various weird interests and appearances. The fact that Alex is the only openly non-binary person at our school doesn't help the treatment they get. It also doesn't help how I get treated for being around them, but I could never leave Alex. Alex is kinda like my dog, Rascal: Looks scary, but loyal to a fault. Not to mention, sweeter to me than anyone else has ever been. Being so close to Alex so unprepared has my brain short circuiting and my face reddening.

"No one! Just thinking out loud." I respond, trying to keep my cool.

"Hmmm," Alex narrows their green eyes at me for just a moment," Arguing with ghosts then? Heard, heard. Well when you aren't on your way to hang out with Amanda, we should find time to hang out ourselves. Catch up. You've been pretty sequestered away since you last ran away. You find anything cool? You go explore the cabin I told you about?" Alex rapid fires at me. Hell, I forgot I'd have to explain things to Alex.

Alex may understand what it's like to not be cis, but I doubt Alex would ever understand the full extent of what I've willingly gotten myself into for the sake of my change.

"Nah, I couldn't find it. You think I'd be back here otherwise? Your sorry ass isn't that good looking." I joke, getting a laugh from Alex. It's a blatant lie, both parts, but the statement seems to not raise any suspicion from them.

"Well," they drop their arms and I take a quick step back against the wall, "I'm sure we can make some magic of our own sometime soon." They wink at me theatrically. This time, I laugh. Alex's teasing always gets a reaction out of me. Whether that reaction be laughter when I expect it, or blushing when I don't. I make a note that the smile on my face also feels somewhat genuine now. Maybe it's just because I'm around Alex again after so long, or maybe the presence of the Maw, but I feel genuinely uplifted today.

"Maybe," I answer to Alex's prodding, "tell ya what, see you after school at the skatepark?"

"Sounds good to me! See ya there, 'Freak!'" Alex shouts ironically as they turn and jog away. Insults being our terms of endearment towards each other. Our way of owning up to being outcasts and revelling in it.they are jogging down the opposite way from my classroom. Did they come over here just to find me?

I don't have time to overthink their intentions though, I have to copy Amanda's homework before the teacher shows. I do however take the time to call back, "See ya there, 'Lunatic'!"

Chapter 3

BLOOD

The day passes with surprising ease, boringly even. The Maw settles down and my ability to go unnoticed plays to my advantage now. I'm at the final hurdles of the day, gym. One class I unfortunately share with Justin.

On auto pilot, I go to the locker room, unlock my locker, grab my clothes and begin to lift my shirt before realizing I'm staring down at teeth instead of my stomach. I throw my hoodie back down and take a quick look around. Everyone's changing and no one's looking my way. Thank fuck I was facing the wall. Stupid! Idiot! I need to be careful now more than ever. "Why not take thy anger out on someone else?" The Maw whispers with a chuckle. At the laugh, one or two people glance my way. I quickly try to cover it up with a cough.

"You need to shut it!" I think at Teratranza, hoping she can hear my intentional thoughts too. I grab my clothes and find my way to the bathroom stalls. We aren't supposed to use them for changing but I do sometimes when I really don't feel comfortable with people seeing my body the way it is. The hair and acne of my body have always caused me immense stress. Not to mention the shape my body is in currently, all boxy without a hint of curve to me.

I take off my hoodie and quickly change into my plain dull gym clothes. I'm glad I pretty much only wear black. If my shirt were white someone may actually be able to see the teeth through my shirt, if this ends up being a particularly sweaty class that is.

I step out of the stall and sneak past as the stragglers to the main gym. It's large and clearly well funded by the school district. Investing more in sports and physicality than the literal mind. The thing schools's meant for. It's idiotic in my opinion, but I've never been one to want to work on my body. Not the way other people do. All I've ever had was my critical, if admittedly cold, mind.

We all wait in various groups for the large form of Coach Alder to trudge his way into the gym. He's always running late. I wait alone, back against the wall, watching the others talk to their friends. I wonder how they can stand it. The flesh they were born into. Being bound by its unchanging nature. How they stand to be chummy, friendly, and cordial with everyone. I see their laughs and I just don't get it. Only Alex can make me laugh, and we are basically inseparable. Even Amanda and I don't see eye to eye much if I were to be honest with her. She usually prattles on about topics I could care less about. The latest drama or spirit week or future careers. All practical and artificial stuff that means nothing to me when I barely feel like I can make it through another day, stuck the way that I am. We just have a lot of classes together so playing at being friends is just easier than not being friends at all. It's not that I don't like her.

She's kind and always tries to include me in things. It's just that she is frivolous in both senses of the word:

She is so carefree and unburdened that I just can't relate to her, and is of no real consequence or value to me, beyond protection from her brother. She adds little to my life and she doesn't understand what it's like to have to pretend to be something you're not. My whole life feels like an act. Do all these people genuinely care for each other? Are they acting? I don't get it.

"How can thou understand those of which thou is not? Can the beast understand the creations of man, or do they just glimpse at what understanding looks like? Then again, Ambitious thing, does a beast even deign to act as thou acts?" The voice of Teratranza startles me but no one seems to notice her talking. I'm glad for the distance between myself and others I usually afford myself. I turn my head away from the others so they don't see me seemingly talking to myself.

"Are you implying I'm less than them all then? Just because I'm different and don't feel the way they do?" Another laugh from the Maw. I feel its jittery movements throughout my body.

"I am saying, Ambitious thing, that thou art more, not less. Wouldest thou say the lion is less than man? Wouldest thou say I am less than thyself?" I ponder that for a moment. What makes a creature more or less than another? Aren't they all just different? Could I even compare a demon like Teratranza to myself or are we just so categorically different, that comparison is useless. She is what she is. Maybe I am what I am. Well, not yet that is.

Coach Alder moseys into the gym finally and class begins. I notice Justin talking to his friends across the way. He catches my gaze as the coach starts to address the class and sneers at me. Dickhead.

"Alright class! Today, we are gonna get yall really moving! Everybody outside! It's track and field day!" Coaches booming voice is nothing compared to Teratranza's the other night. With some groans from the other students, we all begin to shuffle away towards the exits.

After almost half an hour of running, jumping and hucking Javelins, the heat outside as we approach summer is getting to me. I'm normally not bothered by the heat. Hell, I wear hoodies year round, but I'm not typically the most physically active and I am covered in sweat. It doesn't help that I'm getting frustrated. Justin runs faster and gloats. He jumps over some hurdles and shows off. Every time the coach turns his head, it's me getting flipped off, shoved out of the way, or generally terrorized by Justin. Normally he spreads out his bullying but today it seems my earlier defiance pissed him off.

As I step up for my turn on the next event, I hear him making snide comments to his friends about me from the sideline, peaking out around the fence blocking anyone from getting hit by the discus or shot put. We are on discus throwing and my normally numb feelings towards him are flaring with anger. I start to spin and wind up, desperate to beat him in one thing, as he boldly shouts, "Show us what you got, sissy!" at me.

Before the coach can reach him to reprimand, or more than likely just pull him back behind the fence, I feel a tugging sensation from deep in my stomach and my arms move on their own. I let go. I don't even realize what I've done until the discus hits Justin square in the nose.

"AW FUCK!" He shouts as he falls to his knees, hands flying to his face. Everybody is caught off guard, some staring at me, some at Justin's crumpled and cursing form. Some people including the coach rush over to him to help him up.

"Oh shit! That was an accident I swear!" I shout as I put my hands up. It was, wasn't it? I can't throw that accurately. Or that hard. Although that feeling right beforehand of my hands moving on their own? I risk a glance down and see no movement from the Maw.

"You should've been behind the cover like I said! Come on, let's get you to the nurse. Hector! Al! Please get him to the nurses office as quickly as possible. And tilt your head forward, Justin. Try to staunch the bleeding with your shirt or something." Bleeding. Is he hurt that badly? I take a second to focus my gaze on him and see Justin's nose is bleeding as he scrambles up with the help of Hector and Al. He gives me a look that'd normally put me on edge, but I can't stop focusing on the blood. How red it is. How much is gushing from his nose. The scent of it. Coppery but... sweet? I'm so distracted by it it takes me a minute to realize I can smell it from almost ten feet away in an open field. Another minute to hear the coach telling me to take a seat and cool off.

"You're sweating something fierce. Grab some water." What? What does he mean, I'm not any worse than I was a second ago. I look down and suddenly understand why he said that. I'm quite literally dripping, and my shirt is drenched. I'm breathing heavily. Why am I—

Oh.

I can feel it. The maw is salivating. I'm starting to salivate at the scent and sight of his blood. I feel how flushed my face is, the air flowing so quickly through my lungs, and most of all I feel the Maw clenching and dripping saliva. Ready to pounce. I feel ready to pounce. Fuck. I do need to cool off.

"Yeah... yeah, okay." I muster. I walk away with purpose in a wide arc around all the other students who have gone back to talking amongst themselves or continued staring. I grab a water bottle from the cooler the coach had luckily brought out with us. I press it to my forehead. I can feel my own pulse beating through my veins. My adrenaline surging. Fuck sitting down. I need to walk this off.

"Coach! I'm feeling a little better, can I at least walk around the track a bit?" I shout at the bulky teacher. He looks back from the next person throwing, puzzled. He must be wondering why I'm suddenly embracing his class and actually wanting to exercise a little.

"Uh, sure! We only have... ten minutes left of class so just walk the track to cool off! Coaches' gravely voice reaches me on the other side of the field. At this point the Maw is practically gnashing and I make my way down to the track.

"We need to talk." I grumble out loud.

"That we do. Why must thou resist the call of the blood?" Teratranza answers with clear irritation. The alien feeling of a part of my body moving on its own makes me briefly squeamish, but I'm growing used to it.

"It was in front of everybody! They'd stop us! Plus what call? I got a little worked up, that's all. Been a while since I saw anyone's blood but my own." That much was true. I cut my hand for the ritual. I've hurt myself in both frustration about my circumstances and body and in fascination at the sight of blood before. I've been hurt by others many times, but not the other way around. It just took me aback. Momentary silence greets me before a low rumbling laughter that chills my very bones echoes out from the hole in my body.

"Oh.... oh, I see. That is how it is then? My vexation towards thou lessens, Ambitious thing. Thou hast yet to taste the blood and viscera of any but thy own. Thy bloodlust is weak and feeble. Worry not! It shall grow with every lick of blood thou consumes. Of flesh and bone and all things mortal thou tastes. Thou shalt rival my own bloodlust in time." Teratranza assures me like this is a comfort. Sure, the sight of blood has always made me feel strange. I've always called it a simple morbid fascination or a passing fancy, but bloodlust? Me? That's ridiculous. Except for the way my body reacted back there was anything but ridiculous. The adrenaline, the heavy breathing, the fact that every fiber of my being was ready to... to.... I don't know. I don't know what I was gonna do if I hadn't been the subject of everyone's attention. That's new. That's concerning. Control over myself and what little of my circumstances I can manage have always been how I've kept myself safe.

"Are you telling me that this feeling is going to get worse?" I yelp, focusing in on the swirling energy I feel within me.

"Worse or better are matters of simple perspective. Oh, I simply cannot wait to see what monstrous acts thou wilt perform for the sake of thy own becoming." Teratranza practically sings.

"No," I state flatly, "We are going to do this clean. I can't get caught and outed. I need to make a plan. We'll do that together, as soon as I get home. We'll find the perfect subject. Now stop drooling so I can get back to class." I demand with whatever authority I can manage. For a second I believe that our conversation is done.

"Subjects, my darling monster. Subjects." She corrects. Plural. Multiple. Multiple cold blooded, methodical murders to plan. I start to question what I've gotten myself into. Am I capable of this?

Chapter 4

HUNGER

The rest of Gym ended thankfully uneventful. The Maw stopped drooling quickly and I was able to make it to my locker and out of the school without running into Justin or Amanda. Man, explaining Justin's possibly broken nose to Amanda is gonna be tough considering she just told us to stop fighting. Our friendship is already such an empty and hollow thing. Will it survive the strain of this? She's rather useful, if you ignore how envious she makes me feel.

I'm walking now. I walk down the road to the abandoned bargain shop and wander behind it. The quickest and easiest way to the skatepark and Alex is through about half a mile of these woods. Alex has a car so they probably already went back home to grab their board before meeting me there. Everytime they insist on giving me a ride or teaching me to skate, I refuse. I enjoy walking alone in the woods, and I get all the thrill I need watching them. Alex respects that, and I'm thankful for it. The skatepark is more of just where we hang out, since Alex's parents fight with them for not being cis all the time and my house isn't exactly the safest of places either.

I feel the crunch of a stick underfoot and feel almost serene compared to earlier in the day. I've finally cooled off.

However, that has left me feeling fairly drained. Hungry even. Hungrier than usual. Maybe her appetite is getting to me. Whatever. Some time with my one true friend is all I need to recharge now.

The idea of spending the rest of my day with Alex has me in such a good mood that I almost don't notice it as a stick cracks ahead of me. I freeze. Is it a bear? They're usually never this close to town. A figure steps out of the shadows behind one of the trees and into the light filtering in between the leaves. The figure is Justin. Tall, toned, a cruel smile on his face, and his nose is all bandaged up. The hit must have not been bad enough to go to the hospital for. I don't point that out. He's staring at me as he takes leisurely steps towards me. I realize I'm probably supposed to say something instead of sitting here frozen. Maybe I'm supposed to be afraid? I'm just confused though. He can't seem to take the silence any longer and finally speaks.

"Thought you'd be out here. Amanda mentioned overhearing your plans to go to the skatepark when I asked about you. She told me not to come here. To go spend the night at a friends and cool off. I have a better idea though." He says as cracks his knuckles. He doesn't immediately step forward. He's wanting a reaction out of me it seems.

"What do you want? You know that was an accident." I plead as calmly as possible and as sincerely as I do not feel. Wrong response. His face screws up with anger.

"She said the same thing! That I should lay off you. That it wasn't your fault." He steps forward now, pace quickening. ten feet away now. I take a step back. "I told her I just wanted to clear things up." He's in my face now. I can't smell any blood on him but I do smell his cologne. I hate that it genuinely smells nice. That that of all things is what I notice when I'm about to get beaten up. I'm not stupid. I know what's coming. "But you and I both know that's not what I came here for. This has been a long time coming, Freak." He pauses right in front of me, way too close, looking me up and down. Sweat trickles down my forehead. He looks me in the eye and smiles, almost pleasantly. "I almost feel bad." He says with cruel glee.

His fist hits my cheek before I can even react. I'm knocked down to one knee. My backpack falls to the ground a few feet away as I stumble down. I bring a hand to my cheek. It hurts. It hurts bad, but he doesn't hit as hard as my dad does. I can take the pain. I'm used to it, I tell myself as he brings his other fist down on my face. I'm on both knees now. The pain is throbbing but nothing compared to being eaten alive. To living the way I have been for so long. I'll just take the beating and things will be fine.

Two things ruin my plans though. two realizations. As he rears back and kicks me in the chest, knocking me flat onto my back, I realize first that we are alone. No witnesses. The second thing I realize is that not only do I smell it, but I taste blood. My blood. My lip is bleeding. Adrenaline pumps through me. Bolstering me. Fueling me. It may be just my own, but that taste of it makes me feel so fucking hungry. Hungry and angry. Riteous, vindictive fury howls through me. I do not deserve this. He steps forward, not even winded from the exertion. Before he's over me, I roll over and scramble back, onto all fours like an animal.

"What? You're gonna fight back for once? Gonna finally man up? We all know you've never been much of one in the first place!" He growls at me as he raises his fists and circles me. I'm not a man. I'm not even human. I growl back. Nothing but an animal, guttural sound as both me and my Maw scream in unison. He takes a step back.

"What the fuck is—" he doesn't get to finish his sentence before I surge forward. I rise and ram my shoulder into his stomach. It hurts a little but not as much as it has to hurt him as he lands hard on his back as he topples over. I quickly get on top of him, legs straddling his larger form. I raise my fist up and bring it down with all the anger I've never let myself feel. Punching hurts. I never expected that. I've never hit back before. It feels good. Like pressing on a bruise. I keep punching and slamming down into Justin, but his arms are up and blocking me from hitting anywhere important. There's a shrieking noise that keeps growing louder. I realize it's me. Both my mouths, together, howling. Harmonizing my cry.

"GET. THE FUCK. OFF ME!" Roars Justin as he grabs my hoodie at the shoulders and rolls. We tumble down the small slope of a hill. I'm still disoriented and on the ground when he stands back up over me. "I'LL KILL YOU YOU FUCKING PSYCHO!"

Crack.

His shoe hits my sternum. If something's not broken, it sure feels like it. I suddenly can't breathe. I'm retching and choking while he continues to kick me in the face and chest, my arms covering my stomach. I'm on my side. This really hurts now. Through the foggy haze that is my thoughts, I hear Teratranza's voice whispering to me. Goading me to hurt him. To consume him. To take from him.

"Give in, thou craven wretch of a thing! Thou knows what thou must do! The moment is nigh!" It hurts. It's so loud. It'd be so easy to just let it happen. I'm so tired of harboring this pain. Of the abuse I stomach. Of the lack of future I see for myself. So despite my lack of plan, I do it. I let it happen. I let my arms drop away from my stomach. Justin in his fervor and anger sees this and winds back for a kick to where he thinks he'll hurt me worse. No hesitation. He doesn't however notice the upper part of my torso leaning unnaturally backwards from the lower half of my body as the Maw opens wide under my hoodie. I barely have to will it to happen. It's a part of me after all.

He kicks his leg right through my hoodie and into the gaping Maw. His eyes go wide as I slam the Maw shut, through my hoodie and around his foot.

Crunch.

Instantly I taste it. I've tasted my own blood before, but this taste... metallic of course, but the sweetness, oh the sweetness! It tastes sweeter than a thousand sodas! Richer than a million steaks! More vibrant and tasty than anything I could have imagined.

Justin, of course, screams bloody murder. Literally. It almost drags me away from the sensation of crushing his bones and flesh against my teeth. After some chewing, my Maw opens and my tongue drags the meaty bits back into the void in which it comes from. I can hear the satisfied moan from Teratranza coming from my Maw.

I finally drag myself off my side and onto my knees and see Justin, flat on his ass, trying to staunch the bleeding to his severed foot. His teeth are gritted and he's whimpering. My god, he's fucking whimpering. Moving hurts, but I feel good. Better than ever even. That small taste was just enough to get me moving again, but I want more. I stand shakily and begin to take leisurely steps towards him. He's pale. He's shaking. His fingers keep fumbling and they are covered in blood. His blood. Everything smells of his blood right now. There's blood on me, there's blood in the ground, and fuck if there is not a lot of blood on him. A taste isn't enough. Only enough to whet my appetite. Have I been this hungry all day? Have I always been this hungry?

I'm standing over him now. Reading others emotions is not something I am great at, but Justin very obviously looks scared. I can tell he's doing his best to not pass out. He won't stop staring at my Maw. I know the pain he must be in. I let him stew in it a second longer before I crouch down. Elbows on each knee. I stare him in the eyes as I say, my voice hoarse from screaming,

"You taste good." I grab his head with both hands and shove it towards the Maw. Simultaneously my back arches as my Maw opens again. I look down to see his shoulders and back. One last muffled scream is cut off as I lean forward sharply, all this happening in just a second or two.

Crunch.

Silence fills the air as I savor his taste. His blood spurts onto my hoodie and I do not care. I thought I'd feel nothing at his death but I was wrong. I feel a profound sense of contentment. Sound fills the forest again in a daze of loud crunching and snapping as I shovel his limp body slowly into the Maw. Each bite is ecstasy. The sound of slicing meat, snapping bone, and the satisfied sounds of Teratranza emanate throughout the empty calm forest.

I shove the last of him inside me. The void inside me seems endless. I don't feel burdened by the weight of his body, nor does it seem to show on my form. I'm no longer starving, but I'm not full either. It's enough for me for now though. My head begins to clear. I'm sore all over, but not nearly as hurt as I should be. My heart feels light as it ever has. I feel warm.

"Now that is what I call a proper meal, my Ambitious thing! Salty and filling! I cannot wait to try the next course!" Teratranza gleefully proclaims. She starts to laugh, and instead of the crashing sound grating against my ears, I find myself starting to chuckle too. It starts slow but builds until I throw my head back, cackling.

Holy shit! I did it! I successfully fed the demon! I fought off my bully! I look down at my hands, they're smothered in a brutal red. I find myself almost licking them clean. I single thought begins to form through my delighted fever. Blood. Justin's blood. On my hands. No. I look around. His blood is... everywhere. He isn't though. He's...

"Yes, he is dead, thou daft fool. Thou hast consumed him thoroughly. Thou art now a murderer. Congratulations are in order! Thou art closer to thy own becoming than ever! Give him time too... digest. Thou shalt see what thou hast done, truly!" Holy shit. Holy shit! I killed a man! Fuck! FUCK! What am I going to do?! I have to...

No...

Wait. There is no body to hide. The hardest part of hiding murder is taken care of! They won't be able to pin this to me without a body. They won't even know he's dead for sure! I look down. Well, maybe if they find me wandering out of the forest covered in his blood they will. A quick dip in the creek nearby can possibly help with that but what about my hoodie? The massive chunk torn away and presumably consumed into Teratranza's void is a dead give away that I'm not human. It hits me then finally. I'm not just a murderer. I'm officially inhuman. Thank Fuck.

I'm drawn out of my thoughts and back to the waking world as my phone starts ringing from my backpack. I quickly shimmy up the hill, finding that I am not only feeling better, but seem to be completely uninjured. Sore like after a workout? Yes, but not hurt. I check myself, moving and flexing my body, but all I can find is the initial cut on my lip still there. I go to grab my phone, pause, wipe my bloody hand on the tatters of my hoodie, and then actually grab my phone. It's Alex. Fuck, calm down. Calm down. If anyone will notice I'm off in some way, it's Alex. I'm too jittery right now. I feel a little concerned that I can't tell if it's from adrenaline or giddiness. I answer the phone finally.

"Hey! Where are you at? Are you coming the usual way? I'm pretty sure I heard some animal dying in there or something, it was screaming like crazy in the distance. I heard it all the way from the park! Oh I'm here by the way. Anyways, best avoid it the usual way." Alex dumps an avalanche of words immediately. Their enthusiasm is contagious but I have to think straight and appear calm. They heard the screams. Someone else has to have heard them as well then. People might come looking. I gotta move.

"Hey! Uh, yeah, I heard that too. It was a ways off though. I'm by the creek already actually. I decided to take a dip to cool off but had to get out of there when I heard shit." I say as I jog over towards the adjacent hill, which has the creek at the base of the hill just past it. Not a complete lie.

"Fuck, you must've been closer to whatever that was! Did it sound like an animal or what? I couldn't tell? Also, are you good?" Alex's concern for me at this moment throws me off a little. I suppose they aren't aware that I am the dangerous one now. I look back over my shoulder at the bloody spot on the ground where I just physically devoured someone.

"It was totally some kind of dear or something, but yeah I'm fine. Just lost my hoodie though, which sucks." As I reach and begin to wade into the flowing creek, I lift off the tatters of my hoodie with my free hand. I look around, the urge to cover up even with no one around still present.

"Aw damn! That blows. Well, tell you what, still wanna meet me at the park? I can lend you a spare shirt. You know I sleep in my car sometimes. I've got spare shit." Offers Alex which is very sweet of them and conveniently perfect too. I have to minimize the risk of being seen though.

"Sure! But you know I don't, uh, like to be seen without a shirt on... any chance you can meet me, like, a hundred feet past the bathroom?" I ask them a little embarrassed. They are well aware of how much I despise how I look. I think they may actually know I'm not cis either. Jokes on them though, there's no way they know the full extent of it.

"Why not go into the bathroom to change? You've gotta be cold being all soaked from the creek?" They ask with some light concern, "Whatever, you got it! Shoot me a text when you're ready?"

"Yeah that works for me. See you there!" I say.

"See you!" Alex departs. I hang up and put my phone down on my backpack on the bank. I take my hoodie in both hands and toss it downstream. I liked that hoodie but it's wrecked now. I start to quickly dunk myself in a particularly deep section of the creek and get any blood off my arms and pants that I can. Man, wet socks are the worst, but it's better than Alex spotting the blood. Better than them knowing I'm a killer.

Chapter 5

HIDING

Teratranza is being uncharacteristically silent for the latter half of my walk. It's disconcerting, but then again, the feeling of that hunger being sated even a little stays with me, so maybe she's content for now. It's fine by me that she's not causing me any trouble. What little trouble she could cause me right now. That unstoppable untouchable feeling is beginning to fade though, and with it my certainty.

I peek out from behind my tree. I still don't see Alex. That is until they round the corner, exiting the bathroom. The skatepark park is one of the only public places here with a gender neutral restroom. Although, that's just because the people who run the park couldn't be bothered to put more than a single bathroom here.

"Sorry! Caught me at a busy moment! Here you go!" Alex shouts to me. They pull out a shirt that must've been partially tucked into their back pocket and jog my way. When I don't move to greet meet them halfway, Alex pauses. "Uh, you gonna make me come all the way over there?" I quickly nod and they start to shuffle my way again. They're maybe ten feet away from me before I put my hand out from around the tree.

"Stop!" I yell. "Just uh, toss it too me maybe? Then turn around? Please? It's, uh, it's bad today. Okay?" I feel guilty playing the 'I hate my body' card against Alex like this, but I know Alex gets that part of me and won't judge me for it.

"Ah, should've just said. I'd have left it here ahead of time!" Alex states, unflinchingly to my weirdness. Alex wads up the shirt and throws it my way like a baseball. It lands near my feet. Alex dramatically puts their hands over their eyes and turns around. As soon as their back is fully turned I scramble for the shirt. I begin to toss it on as soon as quickly as possible. Alex keeps talking, unaware of the desperation I have to hide right now. "Fuck, am I glad we share a favorite color and band!" Alex shouts like facing the other direction is the same as being in another room. Black and My Chemical Romance. They're not wrong. "House of wolves! Let's listen to that when I drive you home! Does that sound good to you?"

I pull down the shirt finally hiding my new favorite anatomical feature. It is indeed a MCR, House of Wolves shirt. They always remember my favorites. I usually can't get anything by them. Hiding all this will be interesting. I silently walk up to Alex as they hum the chorus of the song. I lightly tap them on the shoulder.

"Now if only you liked rootbeer floats, we could get married." I say sarcastically.

"Just saving them all for you-" Alex's record seems to skip a beat as they turn and look at me. "Damn. You're soaked. Sure everything's alright? What happened to your lip?" Alex begins to ask me, voice brimming with concern. Alex is such a genuine person and friend that it kind of hurts to lie to them. No everything's not alright! I just killed and ate someone and it felt amazing! Amanda will never see her brother again, and I feel almost nothing again! Okay, maybe the severity of my acts had begun to dawn on me during the walk here.

"Yeah. Yeah, I'm fine. I was just overheating a lot. Maybe you could treat me to a float on the way home in a bit?"

"Mmmm... sure thing, lip first though. Did you fall? Do we need to check for a concusion?" Alex interrogates. Damn them and their caring, detail oriented ass. Can they tell I was lying about being okay? Fuck. I'll have to keep my lies close to the truth.

"No, I didn't fall. Just got in a small fight as I left school. Took the hits and kept my head down as usual." I say with as much honesty as I can physically portray.

"That pisses me off. Justin always picks on you when I'm not around. Don't worry I'll put that asshat in his place next time I see him." Yeah, right. I know Alex is about the same height as Justin but they cant just....

Wait.

"How did you know it was Justin?!" I blurt out before I can think better of it. So much for the perfect crime.

"I was right then? Fucker. Amanda texted me to look after you. She got concerned when Justin came to her asking about you and didn't head straight home. Said you broke his nose or something in Gym? Nice job!" They put one hand on their hip and raise the other you for a high five. "Douche deserved everything he got!" I should be concerned. It takes a lot for Amanda to text Alex. Their attitudes towards life and school don't exactly match up often. I can't help it though. I smile at the irony of that statement and Alex's infectious enthusiasm. I clap their hand with my own.

"Damn right, he did. Are you still up to skate some more? You know I'm down to watch and kill some time." I reply. I typically would do just about anything to avoid going home, and Alex knows it.

"Fuck yeah! Come on! Check out this new trick I'm figuring out!" They turn and run off towards the park. As usual, I follow after them, this time with a smile on my face. Despite recent events, or perhaps because of them, I feel great right now! I can't help but smile for once.

As Alex drives us around town, I feel horrible. The feeling of contentedness and lack of hunger had begun to fade, and while all of my real injuries seem to be healed, the soreness of my body is killing me. Worst of all, my new demonic tastebuds have ruined me. Anne's Diner has the best rootbeer floats in this whole boring town, but now they taste like nothing compared to Justin's flesh and blood. they used to be so sweet. Now they're so disappointing. It seems to be upsetting my stomach as well. I put a hand to the closed Maw and hunch forward briefly as sharp waves come and go.

"Hey, don't hurl in my car. I don't care how long we've known each other, I sleep in here! Out the window at least!" Alex shouts pleadingly over Red Leather's Watch My Daddy Die, which is currently blasting over the speakers. Alex's current favorite song.

"I'm not gonna throw up, just something wrong with my float. Maybe a bug got in it or something. Doesn't taste the same." I mutter back in rebuttle. Alex immediately grabs it and takes a big sip. They turn and spit out the window as best they can while driving.

"Nah, it tastes the same shitty flavor as usual. Maybe you finally grew some proper tastebuds?"

"First of all, gross. Why immediately drink potential bug juice? Second, you better watch those words if you want to still be friends after this drive." I mock them through the pain. Either the music's too loud, or I've got a headache forming. My skull feels so full of pressure right behind my eyes.

"Just saying! We both agree it's not great right now. I count that as bonding! You're overcoming your float addiction! Or maybe just coming down with something. Those creeks aren't exactly the cleanest you know?" Another stab of pain keels me over before I can think of a comeback. "Okay, I know you don't like it, but let's get you home. You need some rest. Sleep whatever-" they gesture in my general direction with one hand as they drive, "-this is off." Alex is unfortunately right. I hate the idea of going home so soon., but the sun's setting and I can't really do much right now. I doubt I'm the best company right now, and I hate feeling like a burden to them.

"Fine." Is all I can muster. I've gone a couple days without eating before as a consequence of my parent's irresponsibility and my habit of running away. My stomach hurts in a similar way to that. Like I'm suddenly so hungry my stomach is screaming. Do I even have organs to hurt right now? Not a few hours ago, I just stuffed a body inside a gaping hole in my abdomen. I don't think my anatomy functions like it should anymore. Is this a consequence of that? Dammit Teratranza, what is this?!

I wait for an answer, risking her speaking in close proximity to Alex. No reply. Is something wrong?

We continue the drive with little conversation now beyond Alex attempting to comfort me, windows rolled down as Alex smokes their third cigarette.

By the time I get home my symptoms are getting both worse and weirder. I feel like Justin's kick to my stomach actually hit home but I have butterflies at the same time. My vision is swimming. My teeth, my spine, my hands, and basically every bone in my body are all aching like my skeletons trying to break free. We pull up and park on the street a couple houses down. My dad's car is parked in the driveway but my mother's isn't. She is probably out at the bar already, trying to have another affair.

"Come on, I'll walk you in." Alex offers as they open their door. I'm still unbuckling as I try to argue. Why don't they use a seat belt anymore? Suddenly too cool for life.

"You know what my dad will do if I have someone over." I've taken enough of a beating for one day.

"I know, I know, but you know him. He's gonna be sitting in front of the TV all night. Let's sneak you in the back. I can't just leave you like this." Alex says with confidence. I don't exactly feel up to sneaking, but sometimes there's no arguing with Alex when they put their mind to something.

I get out of the car and creep alongside Alex as he rushes towards the back of the house, quickly outpacing me. I struggle to keep up, focusing on deep even breaths through the deep aching of my bones and rising nausea. By the time I catch up to Alex, they are breathing quite heavily. My thoughts are hazy but that strikes me as odd. Alex was also winded earlier when they cut skateboarding short. It's probably all the smoking honestly.

They've been smoking since they started stealing. So very early on. Alex has always been what people would consider a delinquent. I wish people could see past that to their circumstances and their kind heart and how fully and passionately they live their life. They are kinder and more vibrant than I could ever be.

"Come on," they pant, catching their breath, "you got your key?"

"Uh, yeah, gimme a second." I fish out my ring of keys from my pocket. It only has three keys on it. The key to my house, Alex's house key which their parents don't know about, and the key to my lockbox where I keep all the things I can't risk my parents taking away from me. Cash, my pocket knife, the journal that started all this, etc. The door unlocks with a soft 'click'. The roar of a crowd cheering echoes down the halls from the TV.

Alex leads the way. I stumble almost immediately as I trip over Rascal who was apparently napping at the door. Alex catches me in their arms as Rascal barks and skitters off quickly. Shit. I look up to Alex, who is also clearly startled if their face is any indicator. We both freeze looking at each other.

"Daxton?" Shouts my father from his seat on the couch. His speech is slightly slurred. The sound of heavy footfalls approaches us. Hopefully drinking has put him in a better mood than he usually is in. It's too late for me to shove Alex out the door even if I physically could, so I just reposition myself, leaning against them for support. It feels like I can barely stand.

My dad rounds the corner and immediately scowls as his eyes fall lazily onto Alex and I. His receding, graying hair is unkempt like he had been sleeping on the couch up until now. Probably was. His Penguins hockey shirt has a fresh stain of spilt beer. The offending bottle in hand, he asks, "Who's this?" He squints harder, craning his neck forward like he's trying to catch a glimpse of something distant. Alex, for their part, does not move or say a thing except to look at me. Their eyes are pleading for me to take the lead in diffusing the situation. I know Alex isn't the most comfortable around jerks that they can't fight back against. My dad is not only physically imposing, but fighting him would make things for me much worse, which I know is Alex's main concern.

"This is Alex. You've met before." I state matter of factly. Simple sentences. Nothing to agitate him.

"Hello again, Mr. Meyers." Alex says gently. Like coaxing a cornered animal into doing what they want. Alex is usually bombastic and in your face when it comes to confrontation, but I can tell they're trying to keep me safe.

"Well, 'Alex'," my father uses air quotes for their name, which would feel transphobic if he actually remembered Alex at all, "no guests allowed in the house on a school night. So scram punk." Alex immediately looks angry and starts to object but I speak over them.

"Dad. I'm sick. Alex was just getting me home safely. Can they help me to my room at least?" My father only now seems to genuinely notice the state I'm in. He scratches his stubble with his non-beered hand. After a moment too long in thought he finally answers.

"Whatever... you aren't getting out of school tomorrow, you know?" He says firmly. I nod. "And he's not staying the night." I feel Alex stiffen against me. I wince at the misgendering but my dad doesn't seem to notice as he's already turning around and walking towards the living room. "Hurry up so you can get out." My father calls down the hall. I whisper, "Sorry." To Alex. They don't say anything but start to lead me towards the stairs to the basement. The stairs are in the backside of the house, but it still takes a few minutes to get me down the stairs. The pangs of soreness are so intense it turns to pain wash over me with more and more frequency as Alex helps me down the stairs.

Eventually we cross the unfinished basement, past the laundry room, and get to the small little space that is my room. Alex opens the door and I see the ritual supplies still on the floor along with the journal. I forgot to put it back in the excitement of this morning. Alex's eyes lock onto it for a moment too long for my comfort.

"You've gotta stop staying up late performing spells that never work. I don't care how into the occult you are. At least get some sleep. You're probably stupid exhausted on top of being sick. " Alex shoots me with a look. Diffusing some of the sudden tension I just started feeling. "I'm serious this time. You definitely look like you need some rest."

"Says the person who was winded by a little skating. You never call it that early." I retort. Even in pain, Alex drags me out of myself into conversation. They help sit me down on my bed. Alex's hands are so delicate with me as they do so.

"You gonna need any help changing?" Until Alex winks at me, I can't tell if they're serious or not. I go red but force a laugh, which hurts. I wince out of the laugh and Alex looks at me with concern.

"Nah, I'm fine. Though you should get out of here so you don't get into it with my dad again." It's probably a good thing that my Dad didn't remember Alex as the one who once punched him in the jaw on my behalf. It wasn't even over anything that big. Alex had just had enough of seeing me be tormented by them I guess. My mom banned them from the house officially, and if she were here I'm certain she would remember.

"Okay okay, I get it, you hate me, I'll see myself out." Alex jokes as they turn to leave. They pause though. Eyes glancing at my ritual circle. "Wait, is that in Spanish?" They say stepping closer. It's as they bend down to pick up the journal I realize how close I could be to getting caught.

"It's nothing!" I frantically spout. I try to stand up too quickly and fall back down on the bed. "Just a, uh, book on the occult. You know, another in a million that I've tried and failed with. Starting to doubt this whole occult thing." I lie.

"No wonder it didn't work, its almost all gibberish! Only some of this is in any language I get." Alex says as they hold it in their hands trying to read it.

"Wait... almost? How much of it can you read?" I ask, not able to ignore that particular detail of the remark.

"I mean some of it is in Spanish. And is that... Latin?" They squint at the book, holding it closer to their face. For some reason it makes me nervous. I always forget that Alex grew up speaking Spanish until they're yelling back at their parents at home.

"How do you know Latin?"

"I listen to good metal and loves ancient history. How could I not pick up a few words? Mind if I borrow this?" They ask casually, already book marking the page with the hanging red twine and tucking it under their arms.

"Why?" I ask. With my head beginning to swim, I find it harder and harder to form thoughts and sentences. Whatever is happening is progressing faster. They look at me with a strange and distant expression for just a single second. Long enough for me to notice but short enough for me to question if that really is what just happened.

"Well, maybe I can translate some of it for you? Honestly I didn't get all my books when my parents kicked me out this time. I need something to read at night." I swear they're purposefully trying to sound innocent as they give their reasoning, but their words are all just sound to me right now. It'd be suspicious for me to deny any help with a spell. Alex would know something is up immediately. Plus it took me quite a while to translate enough for a single ritual. Hopefully by the time they translate it, I'll be too far gone for them or anyone to stop me.

"Sure. Why not?" Is what I can manage to say.

"Cool!" They clap me on the back, and turn to continue back towards the door. They stop, hand on the doorknob. "Seriously though, get some rest. Go to bed early if you can. I'll pick you up tomorrow a block down the road, okay?"

"Okay." I agree pitifully. Alex leaves without another word. I lay down and listen for any altercation up stairs but all I hear is the sound of the back sliding open, then closed in the silence of my room. Not even a few seconds later, another wave of pain takes me, and I collapse on my bed fully. Maybe some sleep is what I need. Though I doubt I can sleep through this pain.

I shut my eyes and quickly feel myself slipping away. I suppose I was wrong about that one. As I do though, I hear Teratranza's voice, echoing about my room. I feel my stomach moving as she speaks.

"Sleep, Ambitious thing. Thy body is about to bloom." As she finishes the last word, I'm out like a light.

Chapter 6

TRANSFORMATION

I wake up with the lights still on. The pain has subsided. I try to close my eyes and go back to sleep, but for some reason the light is really bothering me. The dim bulb is shining brightly for once.

I drag myself up out of bed, still feeling exhausted, but feeling less sick. Whatever it was must've passed. I have to shield my face from the light. It's so damned blinding right now. I shield my face from the light one hand as I swipe my other hand blindly at the light switch. I hear the sharp sound of hard plastic breaking and the light goes out.

I pause. What the fuck was that? I stop covering my eyes, only to realize the room is totally dark now, no light coming through the small window. What time is it? No, more importantly why can I still see so clearly? No, even more pressing, what did I just do to the lightswitch? Three jagged lines run at a slight angle downwards across the broken switch. I lift my hand to touch the broken plastic and exposed metal. I stop halfway there. Claws. On the end of each of my fingers sits a sharp, slightly curved, inch long claw emanating from my nail. I quickly look to my other hand. Same thing. Claws. I have claws. A slow laughter builds in my chest. I cover my mouth, trying not to wake anyone in the house. Finally. It's finally happening!

"That it has, my Hungering thing, thou hast finally begun to bloom." Teratranza speaks in a voice much louder than my laugh.

"Shush! Are you trying to get me caught?" I chide. Wait why does my voice sound... different. My T's sound harsher. There's a slight click on certain consonants.

Carefully, trying not to cut my face with my claws, I raise my fingers to poke my at teeth. Sharp. Not just the canines, but everything except for my very back molars. I accidentally prick the tip of one of my fingers. It bleeds gently into my mouth. A slight trickle that stops quickly, but oh, does it taste good. Not as good as Justin did, but still near addicting.

"If thou art done, thou mayest observe the rest of thy blossoming. Thou hast put much effort into it after all." Teratranza sings with amusement.

The rest? She's gifted me more? I turn around quickly, intending on running to the restroom to examine myself. There's a noise behind me as part of me hits my alarm clock, knocking it over. I turn my head back to look and see a spindly tail ending in a sharp triangle jutting from behind me.

"I have a fucking tail?! You gave me a tail!?" I ask Teratranza. My tail begins to flit back and forth like a cat's tail does when excited.

"I gavest thou nothing, oh darling monster. Thou hast taken the reins to thy own life and form, just as thou hast taken the life and form of another." She answers calmly. As if she's done this a million times. For all I know she has.

A question begins to stir in my mind but before I ask it, my excitement gets the better of me. I rush upstairs, as quickly as I can without tearing into everything I touch and as quietly as I can. I can't risk being seen like this by either of my parents. Drunk or not they'll notice something's off.

I hear loud snoring when I make it to the top of the stairs, indicating it's safe for now. As I slink through the house, another change sinks in. I can see in the dark perfectly fine. That would possibly explain my sensitivity to the light earlier. I prowl my way through my own home and make it to the bathroom unnoticed by parent and pet alike.

As I get inside and close the door, I begin to marvel at my new appearance. The sharp claws, wolf-like teeth, and new, slitted yellow eyes are hardly the biggest changes. The tail is the most obvious. As I try to flex and bend it, it proves extremely mobile and precise. The next most obvious is being half a foot taller, more muscular and toned than before. That soreness in my bones and joints.... were those simply accelerated growing pains. This is strange though. Height and muscles aren't exactly monstrous per say. Not that I mind at all.

"Thou envied thy victims strength and thus it has become thy own. What is that phrase humans are fond of saying? 'Thou art what thou consume?'

"You are what you eat." I correct, unable to tear my eyes away from the mirror. I gently take my shirt off. At this point I'm tired of hearing her muffled. I carefully put Alex's shirt on the counter.

I notice then what may be the strangest change out of all of them. The rest I understand, but surrounding the edges of the Maw, my skin is tinged a darker shade of red. I realize it's also the same color on my tail, on my finger tips. There's a tinge of it around my eyes like eyeshadow, and at the corners of my mouth.

"Red as the blood that fuels thee, Hungering thing." Pipes up the demon. Seeing the Maw move as she laughs to herself is almost as surreal as feeling... better. When I look in the mirror I'm scared of all these new changes at once. Scared, figuring out how to hide everything. Despite the suddenness of these changes and the fear that everything is in motion now, most of all, I am feeling better than I ever have felt before. This is the closest I've ever been to being me. The question from earlier stirs up again.

"Teratranza?" I begin to ask.

"What is it thou desires?" She replies.

"How many more?" I drop the question with an intense seriousness. "How many more... blooms. Victims. How many more before I'm... me?"

"That is entirely dependent upon thee and thy victims," Teratranza answers whimsically, "though based on thy current form after one measly devouring, I'd say thy desire and capacity for change art great." She goes silent for a few seconds before finally answering my question. "Two more. Consume two more people thou feels intense envy towards, and thy form shalt be one of thy deepest wishes."

So envy is a part of it? Or at least strong emotions are? I didn't expect that, a f emotions aren't exactly my strong suit. But just two more people and I could have everything I ever wanted.

I wanted to do this as quietly and smoothly as possible but it has all happened so fast and brutal. Maybe that's not such a bad thing. Maybe I should see the fallout of my actions before I revel in them. I twist my tail through and around the shirt on the counter, grabbing it, as I begin to walk confidently back downstairs. I have a body to get used to and to hide. Both will take some work.

The next morning, I wake up to more blinding light, shining through my window this time. My alarm, placed carefully back on my nightstand, is blaring. I immediately grab the sunglasses I set aside last night and throw them on before turning off my alarm. That's enough to let me see without forming a headache instantly so I set about getting ready.

I toss on some black shorts with deep pockets and carefully put back on Alex's shirt. I don't want to have to explain slash marks from my newfound claws to them. I hesitate for just a moment and lift the shirt to my face. I breathe deep. It still smells like them. My heart swells embarrassingly and my mouth waters mortifyingly. Okay, unpack those conflicting feelings later.

"If thou were to ask of me, my thoughts," Teratranza butts in, between my thoughts, "there is no conflict within thee. Desire is simply desire. It begets itself. In that way, thou art nearly as insatiable as I."

"I would never- that's not-" I try to form the words in my flustered state. I gather my thoughts and retort, "Neither of those feelings will ever be fulfilled. I will not hurt Alex or anyone close to me for that matter. Alex doesn't feel that way towards me either..." I trail off. They can't keep a secret to save their life. They tell me everything. They would have said something already. That last is almost enough to sour my mood. That's fine though. I'm used to fake affection and kindness and a lack of either with sincerity. I don't need anyone to accept me but me. I don't need anyone to care for me but me. Wouldn't it be nice though. Just for second? If someone else actually... if Alex actually...

I don't let myself finish that thought. I only need myself, and I'm closer to "achieving" myself than I have ever been before. This is real. I need to focus.

I turn my focus upon moving my unfamiliar tail around my waist. I drive it carefully through each belt loop until it looks like just that: A belt.

Alex's shirt, for once, actually fits me. Considering my sudden growth and my extra height, this makes sense. No one should notice the difference in fit as for my height, well all I can do is hope slouching steeply helps me go back to my original height.

I toss on a light jacket Alex also gifted me. Alex ordered a size too large by mistake and figured I already prefer to wear oversized things. It helps hide my body from people, which is been doing since long before my "blooming" as Teratranza would put it. The sleeves are just long enough to hide my hands in and if I need to, grab things through them. It also conveniently hides how toned my arms are now. The extra muscle conveniently hidden in the folds of the sleeves. Thank goodness I'm used to black hoodies in summer. The jacket won't make me overheat.

Finally I dig up my mask from flu season. All black with a white, shark toothed smile on it. Fitting now more than ever I suppose. First a fake smile, now my real one. After slipping that on, I assure myself that I look as mundane as possible now. I can survive a couple days at school like this. Just pretend to be sick. No one will be the wiser.

Dad's showering so I've got a straight unimpeded shot at the door. I head that way until I smell something delicious and my stomach begins to growl. Literally, again, the Maw begins to growl for a second. Involuntary reactions from it are getting old quickly.

I find myself peeking around the corner of the kitchen and see my mom cooking bacon amongst some other things that smell a lot worse than the bacon does. My attention is locked on the mostly raw, frying meat. She must've gotten home early to be up this early as well. No luck in the affair department I suppose then. Fuck does that bacon smell good. Maybe it's worth the risk. She notices me staring from around the corner and it's suddenly too late to run.

"Whats with the get up?" She asks, eyebrow raised.

"I'm sick." I answer curtly. With how tired I still feel, it's easy to let the exhaustion slip into my voice to make it more convincing. "And I've got a headache." I say gesturing towards my sunglasses. But discussing my appearance with my mother is not what drew me over here, risking drawing my mothers ire. "Can I, um, have a slice of bacon?"

"Sick? Oh, Phil mentioned something about that." She hasn't referred to him as my dad in ages. "Well fine. I made a little too much. Consider it your birthday present this year." She snorts out a laugh.

I was reaching for the bacon when I pause. Birthday present? Was it... had I lost track of the days? I always hated my birthday. It just meant more attention from everyone. Something I dislike from almost everyone. Alex as usual, being the exception. Their attention and affection are the only persons who feel genuine. They make me feel seen and heard. Everything else is just noise.

"Hey, it's not done yet!" My mother suddenly grabs my arm harshly. Her long nails digging into my skin. Shit!

"Wait a second, you little shit!" Shes reprimanding before looking down at my hand and narrowing her eyes. Shit! Shit! "Are you doing your nails again? I told you, this shit ain't for boys!" She shouts. Her hands wrapped around my bare wrist, sleeve pulled back. I accidentally let my sleeve slip down. She's staring angrily at my pale claws and red finger tips. "These press ons look like shit too! Did you try to paint over them? You're so bad at it, why do you keep doing it?!" She's yelling now. Her own nails dig in tighter.

I'm freezing up. Too many moments getting caught doing something that 'ain't for boys' are flashing through my head. I'm sure my face is flushed red with embarrassment. Without me willing it to, the Maw growls defensively as she reaches to rip off the 'press ons'. She startles back, letting go of me. I take the chance to grab the piece of bacon and run towards the door. She's screeching behind me as I sprint.

"I'll kick you out if I find you doing that shit again! You're eighteen now! You can be out on the street for all I care."

I tear the mask down and shovel the bacon slice in my face before replacing my mask. Not filling enough, but juicy and sweet. It's something for now. I can already feel my hunger returning. I have to stay ahead of this. I have to keep myself tame.

I'm out the door moments later. Running down the street towards where Alex will be parked. I'm used to her volatile behavior and to an unloving home, but the words still echo in my head like the ringing of a bell. 'You're eighteen now' and 'Ain't for boys!' Repeat over and over in my head. Something else pokes through too though. The maw growled on my behalf. Teratranza saved me. Maybe the lack of control I have over the Maw as of yet saved me a little too.

"Thanks." I mutter under my breath, knowing she'll hear me.

"Think nothing of it, my Hungering thing. Thou art mine now after all. Not her's." She states matter of factly. This makes me stop running.

She considers me hers. In place of my mothers. Does she consider me...

"But of course, my darling monster! Thou art a child of Teratranza now. Thy change is my pride. Thy joy is my own. As is thy hunger, and much more." She is much more ominous than she is comforting, but comforting all the same.

I'm eighteen. I need to face that. I do things that 'ain't for boys'. I need to accept that, I'm not a boy. I'm the monstrous child of a demon, and I find comfort in that fact.

My birthday is starting out better than most.

Chapter 7

SECRETS

I open the passenger side door to Alex's car. They never lock it. They're still asleep in the driver's seat, leaned all the way back, arms crossed. A small pillow rests behind their head and a blanket is draped over them that I got recently since the maniac would just sleep without one.

I sit down and gently close the door. I lean my seat all the way back and lay down, head turned to look at them. When Alex is awake they're always moving, doing something, fidgeting. Right now though, it's just like whenever they get serious or are concerned for me: a calm stillness. A steadiness to them. A certainty. Like they're dead already and could care less about anything else anymore.

It's as comforting as Teratranza's words were, but in a different way. I don't experience many feelings. Not the way others do at least. Looking at Alex though, something inside me stirs. Something akin to hunger. Adjacent. If I had to name it, it would most likely be desire, as Teratranza had put it, but I could never admit that to myself. Never accept that. We joke and we laugh, but I am and have always been a monster. Just as likely to kill and devour them as I am to giving them a kiss. I can't let either happen.

While I'm a monster, Alex is so very human. Every positive aspect of humanity wrapped up in one spike clad individual. I reach out with my claws. They hover about their face, inches away. I could tear out their throat in an instant. Make a bloody meal of them.

Instead, I use the tips of my claws to brush aside some of their long black hair so I can get a better look at Alex's face. It's stunning. Simple things like a nice jawline and the bridge of their nose look astounding to me. Someone who has literally made their flesh more comfortable for themselves. The same as I'm doing. I sit back up. I pull out my phone and play some music softly until they get up.

I don't have to wait long, just a few minutes, as a sudden fit of coughing wakes them up, panting.

"Woah woah! You okay, Alex?" I ask with concern. They look up wide eyed as they finish hacking.

"Who the-" cough, "who are-" cough cough, "oh," cough, "Daxton, what're you wearing?"

"I'm sick and I have a headache. I think you might be sicker than me though now." I reply. They stop their coughing quickly enough and straighten, stretching as they sit up. They're wearing the same clothes as yesterday.

"Mmmm...., well aren't we all?" They ponder dismissively. "Now! I'm hungry. Are you hungry? Let's get something before school." I'm so hungry I almost say yes immediately, but I hesitate. I can't let Alex see my mouth now. At the same time, I can't look suspicious. Alex takes my momentary pause for what it usually is: A lack of money.

"Don't worry, birthday bitch! It's on me! Been picking up extra shifts at the record store! I can cover it." They assure me. That isn't the problem, but I can't say as much, so I just nod and plug in the aux from my phone to Alex's car as they turn it on. I change the music to something more rowdy. Sleep Is For The Weak by The Dreadnaughts blasts as Alex nods approvingly before taking off driving down the long road, the opposite direction of the school.

I smell something distinct though as we drive. Blood. A scent I'm growing ever more familiar with and sensitive to as well. I discreetly look around but can't find the source. It's very faint. Not enough to set me off, but enough that I have to focus on staying calm. I look over to Alex who's wiping drool and sleep from their face. A small amount of red stains their hand as it returns to the steering wheel. My concern quickly outweighs my growing hunger.

"Hey, you good?" I ask, pointing to their hand. Alex looks confused for a second before realizing that there's blood on their hand. "You're bleeding."

"Nah, that's just some jam from a pop tart I had last night before bed. No worries!" They state. I look at them skeptically. "What? You thought it was blood or something? I freak you out?" They elbow me playfully. I know for a fact that it's blood, but I don't think Incan raise a fuss about it without garnering suspicion. Did they cough it up? Did they do something with the book? I haven't read over all its contents. I'll drop it for now, only because there are other matters to think of. Specifically just how hungry I am now that I've smelt blood. My worry stays with me though.

"Maybe a little," I force a laugh, "but you're right, let's get some food."

We stop by a small burger joint on the way to school. I got a double cheeseburger with extra mustard and a coke. I save the food to eat later, citing an upset stomach. I sip at the coke under my mask and Alex teases me for it.

"If we're both sick, what's the mask even matter?" Alex goads. I don't respond. I don't have a good response. Alex quickly shifts topics when their teasing doesn't get a rise out of me. "So, got any big plans for your birthday?" The caffeine is helping me think clearer, waking me up more out of my exhausted stupor. What am I going to do today?

"Well, I've already been threatened with being thrown out so I suppose surviving the day is my best bet. Do you have any plans?" I inquire hopefully. Committing murder two days in a row may draw too much attention, so hopefully I can hang out with Alex and avoid home some more. Alex first looks immediately pissed off by my first statement, but then unexpectedly looks guilty and begins to rub the back of their neck.

"I'm sorry, I picked up some extra shifts, remember? That's tonight. I'm gonna be busy right after school." They must've noticed the disappointment in my expression through all the layers. "I can call you later tonight if you want? We can meet up in the woods at the usual spot if you feel like sneaking out?" Our usual spot being quite close to the location of Justin's death, this seemed like a bad idea. I shook my head.

"It's all good. I'll probably find something else to fill my time. I probably shouldn't be going out while sick." I justify. It's Alex's turn to look disappointed.

"Yeah, that makes sense. Damn. Sorry. I really hoped I could make your eighteenth as memorable as mine was before..." they trail off, mumbling that last part. Before what? I don't ask about it though, the memories of their eighteenth birthday cloud my mind.

Considering their eighteenth birthday had involved a lot of undraged drinking and me almost drunkenly revealing what little secrets I have that don't know, I'd rather not have that memorable of a birthday. Afterall, I can't let Alex know I'm a monster. Nor that I wanted to kiss them that night, and every night since. It was the first time I'd ever experienced that desire, and ever since then, for months now I've seen Alex a little differently each day. That desire rearing its ugly head. Part of me can't help but ask and tease them.

"Oh yeah? How were you gonna make it memorable for me?" I say in a suggestive tone. Light flirting is normal for us. Normal is good in this case. If things were to change between us... Well, most changes in my life have been rather bad. Except for recently, a little voice in the back of my head argues. Not Teratranza, just my hopeful side. Seldom seen until recently.

"Well, for starters, what birthdays complete without a gift?" As Alex parks near the school, they immediately turn around to grab something from the back seat. Alex's back seat is usually a mess of their belongings. Their parents are always kicking them out and inviting them to stay again. All of their essentials are in this car at this point. Alex pulls out a small cardboard box and holds it out to me.

I stare at it. I didn't actually expect anything from them. They're usually fairly tight on cash. They really must have been picking up a lot of extra shifts.

"What is it?" I say, hesitant to open it.

"Oh, you know, just some flare you've been missing." Alex says confidently, pulling out something from their back pocket. It's a necklace with a skeleton hanging from the cord, arms crossed. I'm too curious now and begin to open my box. It's also a necklace, but instead of a skeleton, it's a coffin. A little "R.I.P." carved into the front. Small hinges on one of the sides glide smoothly as it falls open. A small latch, with the ability to lock it closed indicates it's not broken, just meant to open and close.

"And check this out!" Alex suddenly leans in very close. I almost jump back as my heart skips a beat. They place the skeleton in the coffin and closes it. There's a little opening at the top of the coffin for the cord the skeleton is on to poke through. "They're a matching set! See?" Alex looks up to me, face very close. I almost squeal but cover it up with a cough to the side.

"Thats, uh, sick as fuck. Thanks." A thought hits me. "Wait, you haven't been picking up extra shifts just to get me this have you?"

"What? No..." They lean back again. "I did it to get 'us' a gift." They wink at me mischievously and begin to laugh. "Come one, let's get to class, before we're late. Your next gift will have to wait until you're not sick." They say casually as they get out of the car.

"Wait, there's more?" I call after them as I get out and follow.

"Oh, you better believe it! But it's a surprise! Just you wait." Alex leaves it at that. I may not be the best at reading emotions but Alex almost looks more excited at the idea of this mystery gift than the gift they just gave me.

I know there's no prying any information out of them without guilt tripping them, and I have no current ammunition for that. I'm the one with all the secrets and they've been treating me so kindly recently. More so than usual. I wonder what's up with that, It can't just be my birthday? Could it be because we are both eighteen now..? Both adults..?

I start to lose myself to wishful thinking and daydreams before I'm torn from my own thoughts by a voice.

"The two of thee would go well together." Chimes Teratranza as I start to walk after Alex down the sidewalk. I feel my face flush redder than it probably already was.

"Ugh, why does a demon have to be so embarassing?" I ask, covering my already hidden face with my hands.

"A mother must dote upon their child from time to time." She states simply. "Hey! Are you coming?" Alex calls back to me.

"Uh yeah, I just forgot my food." I reply. I turn around, and open the car door again. I lean down and while hidden by the car, unwrap my meal, raise my shirt, and shove it into the Maw. It's swallowed in one bite. Tasty as usual but definitely missing something. The mostly raw bacon from earlier this morning tasted much better. I grab the empty bag and crush it up. I shove the trash in my pocket and close the door.

"Wait, did you just eat all that? Damn, so much for an upset stomach. You must've been hungry as fuck!" Alex says as I catch back up.

"Starving actually." My mouth waters a little as I feel my hunger being piqued. The Maw demanding something more. Something raw.

We walk the rest of the way to my first class together where Alex drops me off. I don't wear it yet, but I place the necklace in my jacket. I'll put it on when no one will see my hands. Can I even put this on on my own? The claws make it questionable.

"Did you hear about Justin?" I freeze.

"Yeah, he got hurt and had to skip practice, right?" This is coming from some guy who's name I can't remember. Don't think we've ever actually talked directly to each other.

"No, no," says the initial guy. Alphonse. One of the people who helped Justin yesterday get to the nurse yesterday. "He didn't just miss practice. I heard he didn't even make it home. The last person to see him was his twin Amanda. Says she saw him walking off towards the woods and he didn't come home." Oh no. No no no. Word has already gotten out that he's missing. Of course it would, I think to myself, he has a family. You're 'friends' with his twin! Of course his absence would be noticed.

Unlike me.

I raise my sleeved hand.

"Uh, I'm not feeling too well, may I go to the nurses?" I ask Mrs. Morris who seems to notice me for the first time. She looks from my mask to sunglasses, and simply sighs.

"Just go." She says deflated. Clearly too exasperated to call out the dress code violation of wearing sunglasses. Thankfully, I have the excuse of a history of migraines to put out any fires that arise. I get up and leave the class, lecture continuing and no one sparing me a glance beyond Alphonse who seems to notice me for the first time. When he finally registers who it is, he scowls.

"Hey didn't you-" He starts. I ignore him. I don't have time for him or any excuses for whatever he was about to ask. I have to manage a loose end that didn't even register with me until now.

I need to find out where she is and how much she's told anyone. I need to find Amanda.

Chapter 8

DESIRES

I head straight for the restrooms to hide out in until class is over. Missing the rest of English won't be the death of me. Luckily the restroom is empty. I've never felt comfortable with other guys in the restroom, or the changing rooms for gym. I don't feel comfortable being alone with other guys in general most of the time. We just don't click in the ways every other guy seems too.

"I wonder why that may be." Teratranza teases through the Maw. I don't acknowledge her. "Oh come now, why art thou so worried? Not a soul is after thou yet." I slip into one of the stalls and close the door. I lock it and sit on top of the toilet so that my feet don't show at the bottom.

"No, but Amanda knows Justin was looking for me. I need to get a hold of her and make sure she doesn't suspect me. Clear my name ahead of time." I pull out my phone. I can't call her in the middle of class, so I text her, despite the difficulty the claws now pose towards that action "Hey, can we meet up? Heard some stuff and wanted to make sure you're okay." It takes ten nerve wracking minutes for her to reply while I anxiously sit and wait, mildly panicking. The tip of my tail swishes back and forth on its own in spite of the belt loops holding it in place, straining against them. The Maw gnashes its teeth. The ding of her text makes both pause simultaneously.

"It's fine, if this is about Justin, I'm sure he's just too embarrassed to show his face. Heard you're the one who busted his nose. He probably stayed the night at a friend's or something. I got a free block next period though, if you wanna meet up and chat in the library?" A wave of relief passes through me. She doesn't suspect me yet, but then why meet up with her? What is there to chat about? One of our classes? My birthday? Maybe she's more worried than she's letting on? It's probably best to alleviate her fears and keep her distracted. Throw her off my trail.

"Yeah sure, I can afford to cut class." I message back. She quickly answers this time.

"See you there, birthday boy~ ;)" Oh. Oh, that is not the response I expected. Why would she say that? She can't be flirting with me. I faked nearly the entirety of our relationship. She's gotta just be teasing. She doesn't I cant-

"Calm thyself, my Hungering thing. Thou hast experienced flattery aplenty with the one known as 'Alex'. What maketh this one any different?" Teratranza inquires. Her sudden motherly nosiness is going to be the death of me.

"This is different. We're not even really friends. I mean of course I don't want her to be hurt, don't get me wrong, but she knows nothing about the real me."

"Does Alex truly know thee then?" She asks. I pause. I suppose she has a point. I've hidden everything I currently am from Alex, along with everyone else. This doesn't make me feel better though. It makes me feel worse. I'm so tired of pretending. When will someone be able to see the real me?

I pull out the necklace Alex gave me with my talons. I stare at the notch where Alex's necklace fits with mine.

"Its just different, okay?" I slowly and methodically undo the clamp with my clawed fingers and put it on. I somehow manage it without breaking the thing entirely.

"Hey! Whoever's hooking up in there, class is almost over! I'd hurry up!" Comes a voice from outside the stall. I don't recognize it but multiple voices immediately start laughing. How did I not notice anyone slip in? Was I that distracted?

"Piss off!" I growl back with a sudden flare of irritation. I don't usually get angry but something about this situation has gotten me worked up.

The laughter slowly dies, and as I listen, they finish their business and leave. I wait a few minutes until I hear the bell before leaving the stall. I glance in the mirror as I leave the restroom. I look rough. Like I'm trying to hide from the police in some shitty action movie. The necklace though, for its part, looks nice with the rest of my outfit. A bit of flare, I think Alex called it. I like it.

I make my way quickly through the halls towards the library. My stride lengthened by my sudden increase in height. I've been slouching all day to mask it but I'm not bothering now. In the sea of people, there's no way anyone will get a good enough look at my masked face to determine it's me and that something is not right.

I arrive at the library and make my way past the librarian sitting at the desk next time the entrance. There's a seating area used to study, and since it has a good view of the one entrance, I figure I'll wait there. A few minutes pass by of people staring at me like they're trying to figure out who I am. Unable to pin me down or not caring that much, they quickly move on. I begin to slouch down again, trying to blend in. Although no one else is currently at the study seats, so I must stick out like a sore thumb.

Then I see her. Amanda walks in in a flashy and frilly white sweater with black ribbons tied in bows lining the arms and shoulders. The black yoga pants she's wearing shows off and accentuates her plentiful hips in an infuriating way. Her whole outfit hugs her tight, like she's dressed to impress. She looks around and catches me staring in her direction. She looks confused for a second before returning to a smug smile and walking my way.

"You always did love staring at me. Trying to do it anonymously now?" She teases. Gesturing to my glasses and mask. Embarrassingly enough, she has caught me staring at her many times before. Though not out of attraction. Well, not entirely? Emotions like that have always confused me when I do feel them. Do I wish I was them or do I wish I was with them? I get the same way with Alex, but I can usually just joke my way out of it. Right now, regardless of which it is I feel for them, I find myself flustered.

"I, uh, you see-" she waves her hand to cut me off.

"Don't worry, I get it. He found you and hurt you, didn't he?" She steps closer and puts her hand gently to my cheek. "I'm sorry you have to hide the bruises. I told that asshole to not pick on you."

My brain is such a mess at the moment that it takes me a second to realize she's talking about Justin. Her brother. Twin. That I murdered and devoured. I don't know what to say or what to feel right now. Guilt? Desire? Envy? I abandon my established alibi and just agree with her, lost in the moment and her momentum.

"Uh, yeah, he did. It's okay, I'll live." She goes to remove my glasses, but I flinch away. She looks at me with what could either be concern or pity.

"It's okay, I'll make it better." She says with a gentleness. "Follow me, I've got a gift for you." She gets close to my ear and whispers this part with obvious excitement.

She grabs the end of my sleeve and starts to drag me out of the library. I can't help but follow, both out of my sudden conflicting emotions, whatever they may be, and the fact that if I pull away it's likely my hand could slip out of my sleeve and reveal my claws for all to see. Everyone would either take them as the dangerous talons they are or see me with press ons like my mom had. Neither are good options.

With all of that being what it is, I start to question when I began to experience so many feelings? Alex makes me feel things on a regular basis but outside of that and my angry outburst with Justin, I'm used to a pleasant numbness. A lack of any real consequence of consciousness. I don't feel things like this! What's changed?

Regardless of the cause, I'm being guided through the halls, hunched uncomfortably, trying to not draw attention to myself all the same. Despite my attempts to remain unnoticed, Amanda always draws a baseline level of attention wherever she goes. I duck my head down further as people glance our way in the halls. Where is she taking me?

She leads me towards the back of the school and down an odd choice of hallway. I'm confused. There's nothing back here but the teachers lounge and faculty rooms.

"What are you-" I begin to ask.

"Shhhh! Just follow me. Quickly, before we're seen." The hallway we are in is empty but teachers could round the corner or leave the lounge at any moment. She swiftly pulls a key out of her backpack and slips it into the lock on a door I can't put my finger on. Where does this one go?

She opens the door and grabs my arm through the sleeve.

"Hurry!" She commands as she pulls me through the door and gently closes it behind us. Its pitch black in here but I can see it all quite clearly. Stairs leading downwards are all I face.

A bright light hurts my eyes and I nearly hiss. Amanda has pulled out a flashlight.

"Ever been below the school?" She asks, not letting me answer. "You won't find a more private place in the whole school." She emphasizes the word 'private' and tries to look me in the eyes. Thank fuck for my sunglasses or she'd probably be able to tell what I'm feeling towards her better than I myself know. "Still wearing those, huh? We'll try not to trip and ruin that pretty face of yours."

"I don't know if this is a good idea." I mumble. I can feel my hunger as present as my other surfacing emotions, as if my hunger were in tune with them. My guilt is absent now though. I just can't hurt her. That will make me feel guilty again, I'm sure. I've never really experienced guilt. I don't know what to do with it. I want her body.

In some way. I want it. To consume? To look like her? Or something else..? So when she brushes off my comment, I can't help but follow. She leads the way down both the stairs and a long hallway in silence. "Do you, um… Do you explore these places often?" I ask nervously.

"All the time. You don't know everything about me." She turns to me and winks. I don't know how to handle this. What's the proper response? With Alex it'd be easy. With her? What am I supposed to do? She's acting almost exactly how she normally would around me, but I never realized that for all her jokes and playfulness she may feel more for me than I registered.

I measure and manage other people's emotions to stay safe and to survive, but I just don't get them sometimes. How long has she been seriously flirting with me? Did it start today or did I only just notice today? Oh, I'm way over my head here. This is dangerous for us both!

We reach another door at the end of the hall.

"Your present's in here." She says as she opens the door and gestures for me to lead the way inside. Oh, thank goodness. It's an actual present. I don't know what I was expecting at this point. I step into the room. It looks like a boiler room with janitor supplies. I look around as I hear the door close behind me.

"Uh, where's the present?" I ask

"Right here." I hear her say in a distinctly suggestive tone. I turn and am immediately too stunned to speak. With my nightvision, I didn't notice her setting the flashlight down on the floor, and I definitely didn't expect to see her pulling down her pants, revealing bright red lace underwear. I come back to myself just a second later and tear my eyes away from her, covering them with my sleeve.

"WOAH! I, uh, you shouldn't-" I stammer out.

"It's okay, I've wanted this for a while. I know you do too. The way you look at me.

There's a craving. A thirst in your gaze," she remarks, taking a step closer, "a hunger. Well now you have me. Look at me that way again. Please Daxton." Her hands caress my sides, sending a shiver up my spine. She's so close to the Maw that I want to shove her away, but I can't get myself to do so. She's not wrong. I need her. I'm so fucking hungry for this...

What am I thinking? I can't hurt her!

I'm so lost in my inner conflict that I don't notice her hands so close to my face. She grabs my glasses and removes my glasses before I have the chance to stop her. She freezes. I freeze. We're looking each other in the eye now. She doesn't scream. She doesn't run. Maybe... maybe I don't scare her?

"Why are you wearing those weird contacts? I expected a black eye but not... Wait.. Those aren't contacts, are they?" She asks, taking a step back, eyes widening.

"They aren't but it's not what you think either." I admit. I don't know what she thinks it is right now and I don't know what possesses me to show her the truth, but it's too late to go back.

She's not running scared yet, so maybe she can handle a little weirdness. Maybe she can accept me for what I am If she cares about me this much.

"Don't freak out. But this... this is the real me." I take off the jacket and stand to my full height. Her eyes dart between my claws, my muscles, and my face as I now stand a few inches taller than her. She's still frozen, arms wrapped around herself now. She takes a single step back.

Is she scared? I can't tell. My heart is beating so fast and I can't help but feel the need to be known. For her to see me as I am. No going back.

"Daxton... What is this? When did you get so tall? And you... are those-" I pull my mask down.

"Please, this is-" I stammer out. She falls back onto her butt and scrambles backwards. "Wha- what are you!?" Fear now palpable in her voice. Fuck, wait this isn't how this is supposed to go. She wanted me. She made that clear. Is this not what she wanted? To see the real me? To know me? This whirlwind of emotions is so confusing. What's the right response? What's the right move?

"Please, I can explain, I-" I choke out through my locking up throat. Why am I suddenly so... is this sadness I'm feeling? Mourning? Did I just kill our friendship? It never existed in the first place though, right? That's what I always tell myself at least.

"Just kill this wretch already, Hungering thing." Teratranza speaks suddenly. I can feel the teeth gnashing beneath my shirt. Hungering.

"What!?" Amanda yells.

"No no, that wasn't me! It was... fuck, okay, here." I hold my palms up as innocently as I can manage. I slowly slip off my shirt to reveal the Maw. I toss the shirt on the ground as Amanda continues to stare at me.

"It was this thing that said that. I won't hurt you. I- I don't want to hurt you." I promise her. in a flurry of words.

"Are you certain, oh darling monster? Just like you 'didn't hurt' that whelp of a boy, Justin?" Teratranza questions.

Fuck.

"Wait, hold on, what did you do to Justin?" Amanda's voice quivers as she stands, grabbing her flashlight and not taking her eyes off me.

"I... He attacked me. I had no choice, I promise you, it was self defense! I'm not a threat!" I plead. She nods along as I speak, though I can tell the words don't reach her. Her grip tightens around the flashlight.

"Where is my brother, really?" She demands, standing straight, like she's about to take me on. Her demeanor suddenly reminds me that Justin and her are in fact twins. Were twins, I mean.

"Please," I beg with my hands still in the air, backing up as she takes a step forward, "I'm not a threat, I don't want to hurt you. I care about you. I just want to live! I just want people to see me! To care!" The words are spilling out of me without any thought or control. Is that how I really feel right now? Is that what this whirlwind of emotions comes down to? Is that what lies beside this aching in my chest?

"Where. Is. My. Brother?" She asks with dead seriousness. Her hands are shaking but her voice is steely. The guilt floods back. I didn't want her to find out this way. Or at all for that matter.

"He's... he's dead." I finally admit. I turn my head away from her in shame. Crack!

The heavy flashlight hots me in the temple and out of the corner of my eye I see s look of pure, deserved rage on her face. I stumble to my knees, disoriented. I smell my own blood immediately.

Oh no. No no no... but I feel it. The rush. The bloodlust Teratranza spoke of. I don't want to hurt her! This is what she's chosen for herself though, whispers a voice in the back of my head. She'll kill me for what I've done. For what I am. It's her or me. She'll hurt me. Kill me if she gets the chance. The moment the thought occurs to me, I realize it's true, I can see it in her eyes. She saw the real me and reacted with fear. She attacked me. She hates me now that she knows me.

The Maw begins to drool.

Fine. Fuck it.

Chapter 9

ENVY

Amanda winds back again to swing again. I raise my own hand back and swing it at her flashlight as it arcs. I smack it out of her hand and it hits the floor. The flashlight illuminates the room and between the light and my head wound, it's getting harder to think.

Her hands blooms where my claws met her skin with a red that's almost the same color as her underwear. The smell of her blood is sweet and soft like the wine my mom drinks. She grasps her hand and I can tell that the fear is overtaking her. She's a fighter though, just like her brother.

She swings her muscular leg at my crotch and I barely dodge, jumping backwards. I rebound off the wall and pounce like an animal. She ducks. I leap right over her and I land on all fours between her and the door. I'm still getting used to my new height and strength I suppose. I've have to be careful, I need to subdue her, not kill. Don't kill her. You can't kill her. The voice that is my conscience is now small and distant. Thrumming in my ears are the encouragements of Teratranza.

"Kill. Consume. Devour. Become. Stop fighting what you so desperately want!" She goads.

I spin around in time to see Amanda bringing down her full backpack overhead. It slams into my head, knocking it into the concrete floor where it bounces with a sickening smack.

I sit there for a second, unable to process anything. Teratranza and Amanda are both screaming over each other.

"Get up! Kill her! She'll ruin everything yearned for!" Wails the demon.

"You fucking freak! How dare you take him from me! I'm going to the cops! They'll lock you up forever!" Screams Amanda as she throws the door open. She's past me. Fuck she's going to run.

I rapidly rip my tail from my beltloops, breaking them in the process, and whip it at her legs. I just reach and in one go it wraps around her ankle. She falls forward and hits her chin on the ground with another loud crack. Blood. More of it. I'm barely myself now. I can barely think. All instinct. I pull myself up into a low squat as I turned to face her. While she's dazed, I begin to drag her on her stomach across the ground back towards me.

"You shouldn't have done that!" I cry. My eyes are watering. Is it the regret I clearly feel, or the head wound I just suffered? "I wanted to let you live and I still do!" Except I'm so hungry. Teratranza's words just affirm that hunger.

I can't smell anything but her blood. She's next to me now, struggling to drag herself away to freedom. I straddle her and I pin down her arms. I unwrap my tail for just long enough to loop it around both her legs this time, keeping them firmly in place.

"Calm down! Please calm down!" I implore pathetically. I can't tell if I'm talking to her or myself now. I'm shaking and she's shrieking though.

"I'll kill you! I'll fucking kill you! You disgusting horrific freak!" Her words hit me like a smack to the face and fuel to a fire at the same time.

She's right. I'm horrific. I'm a freak. A monster. This is what I wanted. What I want. How could she or anyone ever accept what I am? Why did it have to be her though? Someone who genuinely cares for me? I can see now that she does. She did, at least, until I did this. Until she saw me for me.

I can't hold back anymore. I feel so sorry for her. For what I'm about to do. I'm just so fucking hungry and her blood smells so good.

I bring my head back, and open my jaw as wide as I can. It stretches wider and wider. She's struggling against me but my newfound strength keeps her in place.

I bring down my salivating jaws on her neck with as much force as I can muster. My teeth slice right into her flesh and based on the spurts of blood into my mouth, an artery is severed. I bite down harder and tear clean through.

I toss my head back and chew through the bloody mess of gore I just ripped out of her. She tastes like bliss. Even better than Justin. The Maw starts to open on its own, desperate to consume something too.

I'm reveling in the sole feeling of ecstasy that has overtaken the cluster of conflicting emotions in me. I barely notice her voice sputter out and her body twitching under me. Part of me feels the guilt immediately. It didn't have to be her. Part of me relishes that it was her, saying it was always going to be her.

Envy. Teratranza mentioned it had to do with envy. People I envied. Or that it would speed up the process? I don't know the specifics, but I do know that I felt immense envy towards Amanda.

I look down at her form as she struggles weakly. I pull her back by her hair and lean down. I look at her. Her eyes are struggling to stay open and focus on me. She's gasping for breath and failing.

She has a pretty face. Pretty skin. Breasts I could never have. I look down. Wide hips and an admittedly nice ass in her underwear. Being born a girl wouldn't have felt quite right either. I'd still be a monster. But goddammit would it have been easier. Happier. Maybe I could've felt something outside of jealousy towards her and happiness exclusively around Alex.

All the curves and softness would've felt so much more comfortable than the angles and straight lines of a masculine body. Maybe I wouldn't have even made the deal. Maybe Amanda would've been fine instead of being here, bleeding out in my grasp. Instead of the Maw groaning in hunger. I set her head back down gently to the floor. I lean down further to bring my lips to her ear.

"I'm sorry." I whisper. I pull back and look at her face once more. Her eyes stare out at the wall, unmoving. I gaze down at the body I'm straddling. Definitely no desire now, just envy. Envy and hunger. Thank fuck thats not a line I've crossed. Only murder and cannibalism.

"Thou art not human, my Hungering thing. Thou cannot cannibalize what thou art not by definition." Teratranza says chuckling to herself.

"Can you stop reading my thoughts?" I demand, upset, that she can be so jovial in this moment.

"No. Now, I am simply starving, and I know thou art too. Feast. Now." She demands back. I find that she's right. I'm so fucking hungry, starving, ravenous.

I get off Amanda and step back. I bear witness to the carnage that I just created. Her body is so still. So tantalizing. My tail unwraps from her legs and whips back and forth across the concrete. I sit there for just a moment longer, resisting the urges that are consuming me, out of respect.

I finally give in and lean down. I grab her by the legs, claws digging into her flesh. My upper torso leans far back as the Maw opens wide, my spine bending to its limit. I drag as much of her I can fit in for one big bite. I lean forward and the Maw snaps closed so hard I nearly get whiplash. Slicing and crushing right through the skin and bone of her legs.

The hollow feeling that haunts me being fulfilled is so distracting. So invigorating. I can feel the pain in my skull beginning to clear up already. I could get used to healing fast. My lip still has a cut from yesterday, and I think my temple may still be bruised, but if that's all I walk away with, I'm fine with that.

I drag in her thighs one at a time due to their size. My maw seems as deep as it needs to be but only so wide. As they sever from her body, I have to close my eyes in sheer ecstasy. The taste is unreal.

Unlike the fervor in which I consumed Justin, I savor this meal. Because that's all she is now. A meal. No, says a small voice in my head, she was so much more than that. She is so much more than that. You should leave her body here out of respect. However that voice is drowned out by the absolute pleasure of her flavor.

Due to its size, I have to eat her pelvis in chunks too. The bones crunching as my Maw chews our meal. I sway along with the rhythmic motions in a trance. Backwards opening up, and forward clamping shut. Her guts are pooling out now onto the wet, bloodsoaked concrete floor. A light dripping sound can be heard as the blood finds its way to the floor drain.

I desperately shovel the organs and intestines into my Maw, eager to choke down more of her. I bring some up to my face and begin to bite through them as well. I can't tell what parts of her are going in which parts of me. We blend together in a gory mess as she continues to sink into me.

When nothing is left but her shoulders up, I bend down and begin to gnaw through her arms at the biceps.

I can feel it now that I know what to look for. The aching starts slowly in my body, ever so faint. Her becoming a part of me. Me taking from her. Her form soon to become mine.

When the arm comes off, I feed it to my Maw, bit by bit and bite by bite. Of course I could just swallow it, but I'm committed by this point. Lost in the thrill of my hunger. This isn't for Teratranza, this is for me. I repeat this process with her other arm.

I lift what's left of her to my Maw and bite off the rest of her torso, leaving her head hanging in my hands. Her blonde hair tangled in my claws as her head rotates slowly, eyes still staring out vacantly. I meet her gaze.

That small voice pipes up again. It didn't have to be this way. But it was this way, I reply. She chose this. I chose this. Still, no matter what I tell myself, I feel the guilt that's been eating away at me. The regret. I'm not used to feeling that either.

I take a moment to gently close her eyes, before tossing her head back into my open, waiting Maw and swallowing. I take no pleasure in this last morsel despite the taste. I feel alive, and I feel free, but fuck if I don't regret that it had to be her. She really thought we were friends. Close even, didn't she? Were we friends?

"What does that matter now, my Hungering thing, she's gone!" Teratramza remarks. She sounds almost drunk. Giddy with pleasure. "Thou art but one victim away from everything thou hast ever dreamt of! The envy thou felt towards this one was exceedingly palpable. She wilt make thy form much lovelier than before, I assure thee. Thou shalt get what thou desires."

Despite myself, I can't help but get excited by such a promise. I feel regret, and guilt, and genuinely sad for possibly the first time in a long, long while. In spite of this, I also feel the adrenaline in my veins. The heat radiating off my skin. I feel elevated and more animated than before, as if I were simply asleep until now. I feel good. Better than good. I feel great, amazing, astounding even!

Teratranza has a point to an extent. She's gone. Nothing can change that. I need to look forward to what's next. How do I make my escape? Aw fuck. My situation begins to truly dawn on me. This isn't the woods. This will be found. I look down and see the floor covered in blood. It's sticky as I lift my shoes. I can't possibly lap it all up but the thought does come to mind. The delectable taste of her still on my tongues. Fuck, get it together! You've eaten, you need to think straight! That hollow hunger is full again but I can feel it draining away. I can't afford to get hungry again. I can't escape if I'm in pain either. Will it happen at the same speed? It was hours last time, but I can feel the assimilation this time, so maybe the changes are minutes away for all I know. I need to get moving.

For the moment, I return to my cold calculating self despite the rushing thrum of energy I feel. Take inventory. What evidence is there? Giant pile of blood. Mop it up?

No time, I have no idea when this room will be used next. Wash it down the drain? Maybe.

Flashlight? Stuff it into my backpack. Same with her yoga pants laying on the floor.

Backpacks, Mine and Amanda's. If I leave it here, it'll be found along with the blood and she'll be identified. Better she just goes missing. If I bring it with me, her last known appearance can be traced to me. She already drew attention to us walking the halls though, too late for that.

Bring it with me, stash it somewhere.

My glasses, jacket, mask, and shirt? Taken off beforehand, away from blood. Put them back on and move.

Finally, the blood covering my face, pants, and well... everything else. I washed myself off before in the creek but there isn't one this time. The room has a drain though. Is it just in case the boiler breaks or... There! I find what I was looking for. There's a spigot for water. No immediately visible hose though. Washing the blood off the floor isn't an option.

There's nothing else I can think of to cover and I need to move. I turn on the spigot in the wall, close to the floor. It gushes water that flows into the drain, taking a streak of water with it. Someone will be able to tell it's been used. I'll have to dry off. I wash down my arms first. The blood's sticky, but washes rather easily. That must be because of how fresh it all is. I've tried to clean up dried blood from myself before due to injuries my parents caused or to hide the things I'd done to myself, and it was never this easy. I just need it to not bleed through my sleeves so I snake quick work of it and move on. I don't bother cleaning the blood out from under my claws. Anyone sees them and

I'm toast anyway. It blends in well with my red tinged skin as is.

Next, I quickly wipe down my face and neck. Mostly my neck as it'll be visible. My new necklace is covered so I rinse it quickly as I can, bending down to not take it off. My chest and around the maw are next. I hate looking at my body. Hell if it wasn't for trying to show her the Maw, I would never have taken my shirt off in front of Amanda, or anyone I didn't have to for that matter. Even showering can be rough for me, but I hope that it will become easier with time and change. I drag my hands across the viscous substance, having to go back over it to get any of the small patches of hair I have. I'm thankful, for two reasons now, that I've never been the hairiest of individuals.

The maw is relaxed as I rinse off the teeth. Gently shifting opened and closed ever so slightly. I think I'm getting used to it being mine. Being a part of me. The pale bones feel strange though as I touch them. I guess I haven't really fiddled around with them much.

Finally my pants. They've already gotten a lot of water on them from me washing them off. I get the remaining obvious blood off quickly, leaving a sticky yet nearly invisible coating in places. Thank goodness for black clothes yet again. Finally, I clean off my shoes, which are also, of course, black.

I find some cleaning rags and start to dry myself off with two of them as best I can. I pad them into my pants to dry them off and they come away with some red. It's the best I can do, I tell myself. I then stuff the damp rags into my bag. Leave nothing behind. Besides a large blood pile of course.

I pull out my phone and check the time. The period just ended. I couldn't hear the bell at all, which is a good sign that any of the shouting we did went unnoticed. All that happened in the span of just one class. Whatever, I can't get caught up in it. People are moving between classes now, this is my chance to blend in. I quickly throw everything back on and approach the door, careful to avoid stepping in blood. It's still all I can smell and it's all I can do to not roll around in it, to lick at the pool, but my hunger is mostly sated now and I can focus past the rush of my own blood in my ears. I listen to the other side of the door.

"How methodical, Hungering thing. Dost thou always tidy up after such visceral acts in such a cold and detached manner? Such acts befit a demon such as me more than it does thou." Teratranza supplies.

"Hush, I'm not done. We aren't free yet." I shoot back.

"Thou speaketh to thy new mother in such a way? How unseemly!" She cackles. Good to know one of us is still having fun. When she quiets down, I'm met with silence on the other side of the door as well. Okay. I open the door with Amanda's backpack in hand and book it down the hall as soon as I confirm it's empty. I make it to the stairs without getting lost and step up them as quietly as I can. I can hear the distant footsteps of students as I reach the top.

I try the handle and thankfully it's unlocked. I think I might've eaten the key. I ate a lot of things along with her. That sweater could've been cute... Regardless! I open the door, slip out, and swiftly close the door. No one in sight. I quickly turn the corner and unite with the sea of students. I stand at full height to try and make myself unrecognizable since I'm carrying her backpack, pushing my way through the crowd. I hear some murmurs as I pass.

"Who is that?" One girl says. "I don't know." says another.

"What was he carrying?" Asks someone else.

I move fast towards the exit. I can't stash it inside the school, they'll turn this place upside down and search lockers and rooms when they find the amount of blood I left behind. I quickly exit the school. It's not uncommon for people to stop by the dollar store down the road for their off period. No one bats an eye as I walk with purpose in its direction. My head on a swivel.

I approach my target. It's a big risk, but one I have to take. I'll grab it later. I have to. I open one of the four ever unlocked doors to Alex's car and begin to move their pile of things in the back. I'm not digging through enough to snoop, but enough to bury the backpack.

It's as I begin to move everything back when something catches my eye. I don't mean to look, but why is there a photo of an X-ray in their car? I unfold it and look closer. It's a chest X-ray and there's a red circle surrounding something in the chest cavity. I don't recognize what it is though.

"Ah, and I thought thou was pitiful previously. That poor thing." Teratranza speaks in an almost disenchanted tone of voice compared to her previous enthusiasm. I don't think I've heard her speak this way.

"Do you know what this is?" I ask her. She's silent. "Teratranza, what is this?" I demand. "A pestilence most foul. A thing more insidious than I. It is doom personified. Let it be left at that." She answers morosely. Doom does not sound good. Pestilence though? Is Alex actually sick? I was joking before when I said it, but this looks serious. I remember the blood they coughed up this morning. The coughing fit that woke them. I want to question them, interrogate them, but they'll know that I was snooping through their things. I place the photo down on the floorboard. I'll get to the bottom of this later. They have to be okay. Have to.

I close the door and rush my way back towards the school. I'll be late to class but I'll be damned if I don't blend back in. I have to get away with this. I have to see Alex again.

Chapter 10

BEAUTY

The halls are mostly empty by now so I run towards my next class. I'm still getting used to the changes in my body, but the speed at which I'm able to move surprises me. It shocks a few others as well as I move past them in a rush. I pump the breaks on myself as I approach my classroom and quickly slide in. The room is full of people chattering and idly talking.

I take a seat towards the back and settle in, doing my best to go unnoticed. I get some looks, but the students looking my way turn away quickly enough as the teacher, Ms. Slade walks in, clipboard in hand and begins to call names for attendance. My name gets called and I answer back, "Here." In response. As she's about to call the next name, she glances up, and then takes a good look at me.

"And what is it you think you're wearing in my classroom, mister?" She questions, hands on her hips. Some heads begin to turn my way, eager for any drama in the dreariness of school. The sudden attention sets me on edge almost as much as being called 'mister', and I feel myself getting agitated. Calm down! This isn't like you to let things get to you so much. People call you a guy all the time. I already feel the satiated feeling being drained from me though, and with it, indignation begins to build in me, taking its place.

"I'm sick." I state curtly, annoyance oozing into my voice uncontrollably.

"I do not teach AP Physics so that ill-mannered children like you can disrespect me, disrespect the dress code, or take that tone of voice with me." She remarks. I can still feel the rush of the events downstairs fueling me. Making me reactive. Emotional. Impulsive. I should apologize and let it be, but instead I shoot back, "Actually, ma'am," I start, malice tainting my voice, "As of today, I'm eighteen, not a child. As for respecting you, what have you ever done in your entire life to earn respect from anyone?" It comes out of my mouth before I can think better of it. If I didn't already have everyone's attention, I did now. This is bad, but it feels good to speak up for myself for once. To 'mouth off' without fear.

"You thankless little shit!" She shouts as she slams her hands down on my desk. Some of the students are whispering to each other now. One gasps as her hands hit the table. "I have dedicated my life to teaching. To logic and reason and education. Maybe if your parents disciplined you better, you wouldn't have ended up just like that delinquent you follow everywhere." She spits hatefully."

"And what is that supposed to mean?" I snarl, claws beginning to dig into the underside of the desk as I grip it, and stand, trying to keep a cool head. No way a teacher would imply what I think she's implying. It may be a small town, but to a student?

"Oh, you know exactly what I'm talking about," her wrinkles deepen with her wicked smile. "Teachers hear the rumors too, kid, everyone thinks you're quee—"

The sound of my claws screeching against the desk is barely hidden by the speakers chiming, cutting Ms. Slade off.

"Attention Students and Staff," comes a staticky voice over the intercom, "due to a recent incident, we will need students to evacuate the building. Know that there is no immediate threat, we simply need a calm evacuation. Please make sure to grab your belongings and make way to your usual exit, whether it be bus or car riders. Updates will be shared to parents as investigations continue. Thank you."

The other students begin to look at each other. Ms. Slade looks confused as the rest of them. Only I keep glaring at the decrepit teacher. Calm down. Calm down! She can't hurt you. No one can. It's too late for that. They found the scene earlier than expected, but that's fine. I just have to blend in and pretend I don't know what's going on. At least it's easy to keep a poker face with a mask and sunglasses.

Students are grabbing their belongings and shuffling towards the exits as I stand up, rising to my full height this time, and walk up to Ms. Slade, garnering the teacher's notice. I keep telling myself to stay calm, but I know this anger I'm feeling is right. It's protective. It means something. She has no right to say what she was going to say. So I do something stupid. I lower my head to look over my glasses at her, ignoring the harsh light.

"I dare you to finish that sentence." I growl at her in a low, hushed tone before adjusting my glasses firmly back in place, returning to my desk to shoulder my pack, and walking away. I again don't bother hunching down until I'm out in the hallway. For her part, she does not move or say a word as I leave. I can almost smell her sudden uncertainty of her control over the situation. Her fear.

That was stupid. I don't need the suspicion, but fuck it felt good. I'm so tired of hiding. Hiding who I am. What I am. I feel emboldened by the events of today. People may look at me and fear me for everything I am and am not, but I'll still be me. I'll be more myself every single day. There's nothing they can do to stop me.

"Confidence looks good upon thee." Teratranza states through the Maw. Amongst the talk of the crowd, not a soul notices. "Thou art much more fun when in the heat of the moment and passion. Thou was but a husk when thou called upon me. Look at thee now! Imagine what will become of thee in thy next bloom." It stirs my imagination. I contemplate what more I could possibly earn. So many directions to go, so many things to be. I feel vast.

I can feel it already though. The soreness. The aching within me. Like a sickness yet again. Its onset was much quicker this time around. It took hours for things to settle before. It's been a fraction of that time now. Fuck, I need to get going. Maybe Alex can drive me home if I meet them at their car. If nothing else I need to dispose of the backpack I stashed there sooner or later.

Instead of pushing my way through the crowd, I let it flow and guide me towards the exits. Now is not the time to get a big head and draw attention to myself. Well, more attention that is.

As soon as I'm outside and down the steps, I take a sharp left towards a group of trees in the front lawn of the school. I need to get a clear view to find Alex. I'd text them but my claws have proven to make that a more time consuming endeavor. I have to be so careful to type anything now. The more time it takes, the more time that I could be noticed by any number of people, and I have to keep hiding. Just a little longer, I promise myself. I promise, I promise, we're almost there. One more. Just one more person.

The ache in my ribs and side is growing. I need to find Alex. They're safe for me.

My spine, all the way down into my tail, is sore as I move and shift.

The buses are beginning to pull up and are blocking my view of Alex's car, making coming over here useless. I can feel frustration building up in me again.

These emotions I've felt today are so new. So alien. I can't remember the last time I've let myself feel so much. The last time I've felt so... human.

No.

I wholeheartedly reject the notion and that thought. I'm not human. I never have been. Humanity disgusts me. Emotions and feelings are secondary and messy and cause me nothing but pain. Caring and connectedness are all bullshit that so rarely exists in this world.

Except Alex breaks my views on that. Alex is always the exception. Everything good about humanity, and everything bad too. So very human. So very... everything. Alex is my everything. My eyes begin to well up with tears. I can't lose them. They can't be sick. I have to find them. I start to make my way down towards the sidewalk and the scattered students.

I jog past the buses and see it. Or rather the lack of it. Alex's car is gone. Fuck. I know they said they were busy after school but it's well before school should be over. Where are they?

I walk until I'm far enough away from the crowds and I turn away from them, pulling out my phone. No texts. Not even a call. I shoot Alex a text.

"Hey, where are you?" Gotta keep it casual. Gotta stay calm.

I start walking away from the school just to keep my nerves from building. To lessen the risk of my claws being seen.

Five minutes pass with no response and I'm halfway home. No one's there so I suppose it's safe but, why isn't Alex answering? I give them a call. It rings. And rings and rings and no answer. Just Alex's voicemail saying, "If you're the cops, fuck off. If you're anyone else, leave a message!" Alex's general attitude towards authority has always been 'Fuck off'.

This is unlike them. They always answer when I call unless they're at work. Did they start their shift early? It's a possibility? I don't know what to think. I can feel... is it fear? Anxiety? Something overflowing from within me. Damnit, why do I have to feel all of this all of a sudden!? It's all too much! I leave Alex a message.

"Hey, if you're at work that's cool but give me a text back when you can. I've got a bad feeling about everything today and I'm overwhelmed and I... I need you right now. Okay? Please, just message me when you can." I say into my phone. I hang up the call. Fuck, why admit such weakness to them?

"When did affection for another become weakness, oh, Hungering thing?" Asks Teratranza. I look around, but I'm alone in my walk.

"Since when do I experience all these emotions?"I ask irritably. "Am I gaining others emotions when I consume them? Like how I gained muscles from Justin?" Teratranza barks out a roaring laugh and I quickly try to muffle the Maw with my arms just in case.

"Thou art a fool if thou thinks monsters do not feel emotions. And thou art a fool still if thou thinks thou art wholly monster in the first place." She answers back. Not an answer I wanted to hear. I know I'm not fully a monster yet but I'm trying damnit!

"I have killed for this. I will become as monstrous a thing as I am on the inside. Don't you dare doubt me now." I practically shout with indignation. More raucous laughter.

"Doth thou know why it is I call you 'thing'?" Teratranza suddenly quizzes, sounding thoroughly amused.

I'm taken aback by this. I never really questioned it. I always assumed it was because there wasn't a word for me. For someone who desires monstrousness. Someone who is a monster in human skin.

"Why?" I ask as my sides begin to flair again. This hurts so much but I'm more familiar with what to expect this time. I'm almost home now. Just a little farther.

"It is because thou art monstrous yes, but thou art as human as thou art monster." She supplies.

I slow to a stop. At first what she says doesn't even register. Human? Who? What is she talking about? As what she said begins to click in my head, confusion and outrage begin to stew together. Outrage wins.

"How dare you! After everything I've done? We've done? You'd still call me human?!" I don't care that I'm shouting. I start walking again. I see my house and I walk with purpose towards the front door in spite of my pain. "It's your fault that it had to be her! She could've lived the whole rest of her life!" I shout as I slam my front door closed. I don't see him but I hear Rascal skittering away from the sound of me as I raise my voice.

"I do not deny my role in cutting the strings of her life short, nor in fueling thy change. Here me now and hear me well, my darling creature." Teratranza commands. "There art monstrous humans who perform acts far more vile than death. There art monsters who act with humanity and compassion. Thou art neither. I have seen thy very soul. Thou art something new. Thou art my child now, and thy final bloom shall give birth to my ultimate, beautiful creation!" Her words shock me, but rage is winning in me right now. All I feel is indignation.

What beauty is there if not a true monster? What could possibly be beautiful when she once called me pitiful? Neither human nor monster? What does that leave?

"And what will my final 'bloom' create? What's so beautiful if I'm not a monster then, demon?" I practically spit at her. I'm shaking and breathing heavily. The pain is immense and I'm losing my ability to stay focused. I can feel myself struggling to stay conscious. I'm moving towards my room. I can't let this happen in the open. I don't know how long it'll take.

She answers me with quite possibly the kindest and most heartfelt tone I have ever heard from any living thing.

"Thy final bloom shall finally create Thou. As thou hast always meant to be. As thou hast always envisioned. And thou art beautiful, my child."

My legs give out, and I fall down the stairs. My last thought as I try and fail to catch myself tumbling down is, "Oh. She thinks I'm beautiful?"

My head it's the floor.

Chapter 11

AWAKENING

I wake up in a heap on the floor. I can't tell what time of day it is.

My head is pounding. Here I thought the pain would be over when I afterwards.

I must've done something wrong as I tried to catch myself because my arms ache. I take a second to just sit there in a miserable pile of splayed limbs.

Okay, enough self pity. Get up time. I don't budge. Come on, let's go. Nothing but my body aching from the fall. Okay, a few more minutes.

I lay there on my stomach, slowly coming back to myself. I feel like shit, but I can tell that's more from the fall than anything else. The transformation pain is gone.

Everything Teratranza said comes back to me, slowly, as I begin to be able to form cohesive thoughts.

Beautiful. She thinks I'm... that I'll be..?

I don't know what to say. If I'm not a monster, then what am I? If I begin to feel more and more in line with my humanity as I transform myself, what will I become? 'You' is what she answered before. Well, close enough. I'll become me. I guess I'm starting to wonder who that is.

It's been a few minutes and I've heard nothing from upstairs, so it must still be early in the day. School did evacuate pretty early on. With no one home, I should be free to move about the house without caution.

Alright. This time, for real. I begin to pick myself up, and immediately I notice the first and biggest change. My arms. I thought they felt sore from the fall but I was wrong. They felt sore from growing.

I look down to see two pairs of arms. Four in total. Holy shit! I take a glance at my sides and see where my ribs were aching, I've sprouted new arms, identical to my original ones. The new arms each end with a set of wicked looking claws, same as the other set. They've ripped through the shirt Alex gave me like they emerged with force. Fuck. That was important to me and I can't explain those holes to Alex.

That's when I notice that the shirt is ripped in several places. As are my pants. My larger jacket fits me snuggly now. Did I have another growth spurt? But if that were all, then why does my body feel... off? Not bad, beyond the pain, but different. The clothes pull tightly against my body in odd places. Fuck it. I'll shower and get a new set of clothes in a minute. First I need to see what else has changed.

I'm sitting now, studying my arms. They're muscular but lithe. Hairless as well for some reason. The skin is smooth as I drag one of my four hands across the biceps of one of my new arms. New arms. Man, this is wild! I almost can't believe it, but so much has changed in these past few days, my astonishment quickly changes to contentment. I like them. I like this change.

Beyond the arms and my sudden growth, I can't seem to tell if anything else has changed. Not that those wouldn't be enough for me. New arms are a big change.

The red on the tips of my fingers has spread down to the base of them.

My head feels heavy from when it smacked the floor. Wait, I was wearing my glasses when I fell. I look up to see the broken glasses. I didn't really realize they were missing with how dark it is downstairs already, but that fall must've shattered them.

As I turn my head I swear I see something out of the corner of my eye, but when I turn, there's nothing. My head must be more messed up than I thought.

I pick myself up and bump my head against the ever so low ceiling. Ow. I must be well over six feet tall now to have that happen. I toss off the jacket, since it's the one piece of clothing that hasn't been ruined yet. It's an awkward and strange feeling as I do so. I don't know what to do with my extra limbs yet.

"Anyone home?" I call up the stairs. The only response is Rascals barking.

I'm alone then, so I figure I'll shower first, then bother grabbing clothes. I want to check myself out in the mirror anyway. I hunch down to make my way up the stairs, using my 4 arms to stabilize myself against the walls as I climb multiple steps at a time. I quickly reach the top of the stairs and squint at the bright light pouring through the windows. Nearly blind, I feel my way down the halls, looking down, careful not to step on Rascal wherever he is.

I make it to the restroom and quickly turn to shut the door. Total darkness. I can finally see again. I turn to the mirror and am shocked by what I see next.

First of all, I have horns. Pitch black horns like that of a ram's growing from where my temples meet my forehead, curving up, backwards, and ending jaggedly pointing forward. My head doesn't feel heavier from any injury. It feels heavier from these! Through my peripheral vision I can see them just barely, poking sharply towards the mirror. My skin around them as well as the base of them is the same deep red as the discoloration surrounding my other changes.

The second change I see is why my clothes don't feel like they fit quite like they should. The tears in them aren't just from growing taller. But that can't be. My hips and chest are... no way. Did I..? Am I...? I can't stand it anymore, I have to see it in full. I start to try and take my shirt off before realizing how difficult that is with four arms. Shirts aren't exactly made for four limbs.

I start to feel impatient and frustrated, so I begin tearing away at my already ruined clothes with my twenty razor sharp claws. Not just the shirt but the pants as well. Where there were tears and rips before, there are now tattered remains that fall to the ground. Sorry about the shirt Alex but...

Holy. Shit.

I see myself with features I could have only dreamed of possessing myself. My hips aren't as wide and plentiful as Amanda's were but they're absolutely more... feminine. My thighs as well. Much larger. Both fat and muscle leave them plump.

Where before, my chest was absolutely barren, now sit breasts. I don't know much about cup sizes but they're smaller and I am astounded by them.

My smaller patches of chest hair are gone. In fact all my body hair is gone. I hug myself with all four limbs as tears well up in my eyes and I drag my hands along my newly smooth skin.

My hair is still shorter, but my face is gentler. Still sharp at the cheekbones and chin, but even those only compliment the more feminine look. I look…

"Beautiful?" The Maw supplies. Teratranza's voice comes through with a hint of the same softness she spared me during my outburst. "Thou always have been. Now thou simply align more with how thou hast always been within." I don't know how to respond.

I can feel my tail whipping back and forth. I can feel a cry building behind my eyes.

When was the last time I actually let myself cry? Have I ever cried from joy? Who cares? I let the tears flow, and a sob wail from my lungs as I struggle to stay standing. My knees tremble and I have to use all my arms to catch myself on the counter.

I don't have all of Amanda's features, and I'm much more muted in them than she was, but I look like a monstrous woman instead of a monstrous man. And oh god does it feel good. Like a vise around my heart being released. One that's always been there. So long that it grew nearly imperceptible. Buried.

I wipe the tears from my eyes with the back of my hands. I stand there, gazing into the mirror and taking it all in.

Sharp yellow eyes stare back. I'm over six foot tall, curved and muscular. A giant toothy maw on my stomach sitting below my lovely new breasts and above hips I could only ever envy in others. Four toned arms ending in sharp talons all move in unison as I flex them. A pointed tail whipping back and forth around me. I can't help but smile like an idiot looking at myself. Sharp interlocking teeth greet me in that grin. Dark ridged horns protrude from my skull as darker hair falls just past them. My eyes are red and puffy but my face, while still noticeably me, has an elegance to it that it never had before.

I'm not the monster I've always felt within me, but I'm close. I'm so close and fuck does it feel good.

I guess feeling things isn't always so bad. Maybe humanity isn't so bad if this is what it's like to feel... I don't know what to call it. I do know that it's unlike the ecstasy of devouring someone, losing myself to the call of blood. This is gentler, softer, and more joyous and cheerful than I have ever felt before!

I turn around to get a casual look at my ass to see if that's also developed some and get yet another shock.

All along my spine starting at my nape, are small sharp looking spikes. Fiendish spines line my back all the way down to nearly the end of my tail. Those particular spines were so small I didn't notice them but they look like they could do some damage if I'm not careful with my tail now. Or if someone were to come at me.

No more hiding my tail in my belt loops. Hell, only a few of my clothes could possibly fit now. All the oversized stuff I used to wear to hide my body from people. But still, there's no hiding... all of this! I just can't get over how amazing it feels to look this way. To be this way!

I'm going to have to get used to a lot of things though. No more sleeping on my back, which never really was a problem in the first place, but also no more going out in public as Daxton. Anyone who could possibly recognize me still would know something's off. That's if anyone can still recognize me.

My mind wanders as I begin to turn on the shower's hot water.

My parents are the most immediate risk. Will they see their son turned monster? Or this 'thing' I am now having invaded their home? I have no place here anymore. I'll gather what I might need before I leave. To where, though, I don't know yet.

As the water hits my skin, remnants of red dribble off me and down the drain. The heat feels good. Not the gentle comforting good I normally go for, but in a 'almost hot enough to burn' kind of way. Like stretching the soreness out of you after a workout. Like pressing a little too firmly on a bruise.

All the tension I've been holding seeps off me as the water cascades down my form. I watch it flow down me, mesmerized.

The Maw, for its part, stays closed and unmoving. I guess drinking shower water wouldn't be pleasant.

I probably shouldn't go anywhere too public anymore unless I have to. Even with new clothes, I doubt anything could really hide all these changes. Having no sunglasses anymore and having literal fucking horns are kind of a dead give away regardless of how oversized of an outfit I manage to find. I wrap my lower arms around myself tightly to see if they would even look convincingly not there.

This fails miserably. Okay, with my eyes and the danger of being in public, I should only really roam around at night. I have to, however, leave the house before dark and before my parents get home.

I'm just standing there now, having scrubbed my new body clean with efficiency only four arms can provide. I brush my hair back with my top left hand. I lean forward and let the hot water run down my back as I let myself approach a topic I've been avoiding thinking about.

Alex.

Everything I've said should apply to Alex too. They're my best friend, my closest companion, and everything I can afford to care about that isn't just myself anymore.

None of that changes the fact that they may not recognize me anymore. Even if they did, why would they accept me? If it was just me expressing myself in a more feminine way, then Alex would understand it. These changes have been so sudden though, and they don't stop at making me more femme presenting.

Images of Amanda's face in the dark of that room flash through my head. Shock, confusion, unease, anger, and fear. The sudden and rapid decline of me in her eyes. She was willing to do so much, but not accept me. Will Alex be the same? Is Alex only close to me until I push too far? I'm even more monstrous than I was before with Amanda.

Would they be happy for me if I could just explain it? They have the book. They've probably looked through it. I could tell them that I lied and it actually did work. Phenomenally so. Alex knows the joy that comes with realigning your body to be more yourself than anyone else possibly could.

I'm beautiful, right? Alex can accept beautiful, I'm sure. They have to. I can't lose them too. I'm giving up everything I ever had for this, and I will gladly pay any price, but I can't give them away too.

My home, my family, my dog, my school life, any future jobs, any future love or connection. I'm going to be losing all of those for the sake of myself. Sacrificing myself, to myself. This is what that meant, right? Losing all connections to the old me, becoming the new me.

Who am I though without Alex? Alex is as much a part of me as my monstrousness is, not just not just another connection to my old life. They are a very part of my soul. I feel that now. I'm allowing myself to feel what I've always felt and I know it to be as true as I am now.

I love Alex.

Did it start when I almost kissed them on their birthday? When Alex stood up for me getting bullied the first time? When Alex and I first sang MCR in the car together? I don't know. All I know is I have to find them again. At least one last time. I'm already too far gone and need to disappear. One more person still has to die. To be subsumed into myself. I can't involve Alex in this, but I can't leave without saying goodbye.

Earlier events come to mind and I realize I've already involved them. The evidence to a murder is in their back seat wherever they are now, under all that garbage and clothing.

Only now do I notice the water having turned cold against my skin. I turn it off and hear something. A small muffled 'ding' noise. My phone! It's still in those pants.

I don't bother toweling off or turning off the water. I scramble out of the tub and dig for my phone in the tattered rags on the floor. I pause only long enough to wipe my top pair of hands off so as to not get my phone wet. It's a text. From Alex no less. I notice two missed calls as well. I frantically open the text and read.

"Hey Dax, things are hectic right now, but I went home to grab some stuff while I thought my parents wouldn't be home. Sorry for bailing!" This message is sent first, followed by the two call attempts. "Look though, we need to talk. This is hard to say but I know you've been keeping something from me. I've also been keeping something from you. So I suppose we're both guilty in that regard. I'm not gonna lie, shit's serious, but I think you might know that already. I lied about the extra shifts tonight. Sorry. I'm headed to the cabin I told you about before. Meet me there by sunset tomorrow. Already headed that way now. I hope I'll get to see you."

I'm on all fours, with my fifth and sixth limbs clutching my phone. Alex knows something is up. Alex is onto me, but they were also being super cryptic. Just how much do they know? Is their own secret their illness or something more? Why meet there? I have so many questions.

I immediately try to call them but it goes straight to voicemail. I try again. A third time. A fourth. No ringing, right to voicemail. All the tension that had left my body returns as I make these frantic attempts to reach them.

My phone screen cracks as I accidentally grasp onto it a little too tight. Fuck! Their phone must be off, but why? This is so nerve wracking that I just squeeze my phone like a stress ball. It completely shatters as I crumple it into a literal stress ball.

I drop it to the ground, letting the small cuts on my hands flow. The scent of blood. It raises my adrenaline further but this allows me to narrow in to focus. I lick my palms and swallow. Blood and glass both. I feel my senses sharpen as if going in for the kill. No thinking. Just Instinct. I need Alex.

Chapter 12

DEPARTURE

I rush out of the room, practically slamming my way through the door as I hurry across the house to my room.

"What is it thou plans on doing now?" Inquires Teratranza, her calm tone contrasting my fevered pace.

I dive down the stairs, landing on all six limbs. I feel the impact like it's just a weak slap.

I'm running across the basement to my room, arms each grasping at the walls and ceiling to propel me faster.

I finally get to my room and literally slam into the door this time. Fuck it! No time!

The entirety of the door cracks and crumbles as I force my arms through the holes that were made and bust the rest of it open. I feel feral. Out of control.

When I'm finally standing in the center of my small room hunched over, I find myself lost in the thrum of blood in my veins. Where's the blood? I can taste it. Where is it? What was I doing? What was so important..?

It takes me standing there for several seconds to realize Teratranza is speaking.

"—need to calm thyself. Thou art nearly insatiable in thy lust for blood now. It will become thy sole motivator soon if thou were to lose thyself in the mania of hunger."

I pause to process her words. I can feel that 'lust for blood' urging me to move, but I know I have something to do…

I look down to see a little metal coffin dangling from my neck. Alex!

"Oh good, thou art paying attention. Now, my Monstrous Thing, what art thy plans?" She asks in a composed manner.

Her question pulls my focus enough to keep me from hunting for imaginary victims. What are my plans? Find Alex? No, before that. My room? Gather my things. Oh yeah, this is the last time I'll be here isn't it? That realization hits me harder now. Whatever I leave behind here will stay gone. Forever.

Good, I find myself thinking.

"Gather what I need. Clothes and essentials. Find Alex." I finally answer Teratranza. "And what then?" She demands coolly. I don't answer. "Thou hast not the slightest of ideas, does thou?" I shake my head.

"Doesn't matter. Whatever happens, happens. I just need to find Alex first. It'll all be okay." It has to be, I tell myself. I get no reply from Teratranza.

My breathing is still labored but I set about finding what I need. I don't have any underwear that'll fit me anymore I realize. So I just find my only pair of stretchy joggers and begin to shimmy my legs through. The feel and fit are totally different from before. When they're fully on, I lift and stretch my legs, but they don't burst at the seems like I'd expect from any other pants I own. They sit on me in a flattering way and I note a distinct feeling of euphoria as I go about searching for my next find.

A Babymetal Hoodie, borrowed from Alex as well. Oversized on them, so should just fit me? I hope it does at least. First things first though, I use my open hands as measurements to determine where to cut. Sorry Alex, I'll make it up to you.

I use my claws to roughly cut the hoodie into a crop top. Just enough to cover my new chest, but not the Maw or my new arms as they rest at my sides. No more hiding. This is me. I've covered up enough. It fits me snuggly, and If I lift all my arms it almost flashes, but I'm definitely in the clear there.

I then grab the only other things that matter to me in this room. The first, a polaroid of Alex and I on their eighteenth birthday, hanging above my bed. It's a selfie taken by Alex. Alex's eyes look right into the camera and they're grinning like an idiot. For my part, I am also facing the camera, but my gaze is shifted out the corner of my eyes to stare at Alex's face. We were both drunk in the photo, and both so close.

This was the moment I almost kissed them. The moment I've felt conflicted about ever since, but right now, all I feel is regret for not having done so sooner. For losing my chance tk do so. I stuff the picture in my pocket, hoping I won't lose it as I run. Luckily, the pockets have zippers, which I carefully zip closed.

The second and final item I grab is my lock box. I rip open the metal container easily, no longer needing to hide its contents.

Alex has the Journal. My parents can find my spell materials and my knife for all I care. I grab the one thing I hadn't touched since my last beating from my father. A small, bright red ribbon I bought thinking I'd one day use it to put my hair up in a nice style when my hair eventually grew out a bit more.

My father found out about it, and while he wasn't able to take the ribbon from me, he did leave me a crumpled mess on the floor. He'd gotten really good over the years at detecting any hint of my more feminine desires. He'd also gotten good over the years of not leaving any marks visible on me while I'm in public. Hits to the gut, kicks to my legs, fists slammed into my head where my hair covers. He'd gotten good at making me hurt. No longer.

I use one set of arms to hold the back half of my hair in place, and the second pair to tie the ribbon into a bow, putting my hair onto a nice half pontytail. It may look silly. For all I know it could look like a mess, but it feels freeing to do so and I'll chase that feeling as long as I live from here on out.

I'm just standing here now. My eyes have begun to adjust to the bright light of day peaking through my window. The sun must be getting close to setting. I don't have the time on me anymore due to my crumpled and destroyed phone.

I look around at the room I'll never return to. A room full of bad memories. A room where my life changed. Something boils up inside of me and I begin to rip the place apart, slashing my claws into my pillow, the walls, and my wardrobe. Everything I can reach with all four limbs from the center of my room.

By the time I feel satisfied, the place looks like a whole pack of wolves threw a rager. Good. My mark is left, and nothing of value is here anymore. Only out there, in the woods right now, is there anything I care truly about.

I exit the remnants of my room and calmly walk myself up the stairs. Rascal sees me from across the hall and runs up to me, excited and wanting pets. One last time, I think.

I carefully bend down and rub my open palms across him. I don't wanna risk hurting him, but he seems to enjoy being petted by four arms all at once.

I then go and simply open the back door. He's bolts for his opportunity for freedom. He's better off fending for himself than in this household without me. I care about Rascal enough to want him to be okay, but not enough to stay for him. I couldn't leave him to them and their abuse.

Goodbye little buddy.

It's as I stand by the open back door, staring out at the forest line just past the broken fence Rascal easily jumps through, that I hear the creak of the front door open. I quickly turn to see my Father staring at me, frozen.

What must I look like to him, I wonder. A monster? His 'son'? Something out of this world that broke into his home. He'd never see me for the woman I am, that's for sure. I find that I'm not scared of him in this moment. He can't hurt me.

"Hello Father." I greet him calmly.

"W-what!?" He stammers out. "You're not- you can't be- what are you!?" He's slowly reaching for the bat he keeps by the front door for home defense. I let him. I don't answer. I just sit there, staring daggers at him.

He firmly grasps the bat and I see his confusion and fear give way to anger on his face. "GET OUT OF MY HOUSE!" He yells as he comes forward swinging. My reach is longer than his though and as soon as he is close enough I grab his wrist mid swing, stopping hisnswing with ease. He stares at me, flabbergasted.

I'm taller than him now, I note as I quickly twist my hand, breaking his arm with an audible snap. He cries out and falls to his knees. I grab his thinning hair and drag him up to his feet. He doesn't get to back away from this. I stare unblinking into his eyes. I get so close I can smell the putrescene that is his breath.

"You can never harm me again, but I can and will harm you for all you've done." I muster in the calmest tone I can manage, anger clearly leaking through.

His eyes are darting back and forth between my features now as he struggles to make me release him.

His strength is... nothing now, I find. I've grown beyond him. Beyond his capacity to minimize and hurt me.

"Lucky for you I have more important things to deal with," I hiss at him, "but mark my words: I will come for you. Know that it will hurt. Know that it will only be a fraction of all you've done to me. Know that I can kill you, anytime I want, and oh, do I want to. You skip town and I'll hunt you down. Till then, you're nothing but a walking corpse." I warn him through now gritted teeth. He snivels all the while throughout my declaration of his death.

I drop the coward in a crumpled mess on the ground. He cries out again as he hits the ground hard, and begins to clutch the arm I broke.

"Get your affairs in order." I casually call behind me as I turn and begin to run out the open door.

I'm able to run faster than I ever have been. The rush of wind on my face as I leap over the fencing and disappear into the woods feels like deliverance from all that house meant. All he meant. The looming threat of being forced to conform to a predestined role is gone now utterly. I am more than that. I am free.

"Are you sure letting him live was wise? A cornered and afraid animal fights ever harder." Teratranza advises.

"Alex is more important. He dies as soon as I know they're safe." I reply.

"Wilst thou eat him?" She questions. I don't know what I'm going to say until it leaves my mouth but every word rings true.

"There's nothing to be gained from eating trash. Nothing about him is appetizing or enviable. His corpse will rot." I state coldly.

Malice. That's another new one, but I feel it strongly. I'm getting used to these emotions I think. From the violent, righteous anger I feel towards how I've been treated throughout my life, to the joy and relief I feel due to being myself. The freedom that comes with it all.

As I'm running through the woods, I barely feel winded. This new form is ever more stronger and more capable than ever it seems.

I stumble just as I think that, but catch myself with my four arms and instinctually begin to gallop across the verdant forest floor. It feels as natural as running does. My claws dig into the dirt as I propel myself forward.

Don't stop moving. Never stop moving. I have to find Alex. I just need to figure out how to track him. He can't have gotten that far, and I'm traversing the forest much faster than I ever could before. I could probably reach the cabin tonight if I keep this up.

With how fast the trees are flying by me, I feel like I have to be galloping at speeds only a horse could possibly reach, except I'm doing it over harsh and rough terrain instead of open plains.

I feel unstoppable and nervous at the same time. Nothing I can imagine could possibly stop me physically anymore, but if Alex were to see me and be horrified, or even run in terror, I'd be devastated beyond belief.

Amanda was afraid. My dad was afraid. Even Justin was at the end. Who wouldn't be afraid of me now? I press forward nonetheless, nerves only building worse and worse.

The sun has just about finished setting. Trickles of twilight filter through the canopy above me. I've taken the long way around to where I originally set off towards the cabin to begin this whole mess.

I start heading towards that direction. This is the most likely path Alex would have taken. The one they described when they told me the rumors about the cabin in the first place.

I'm a mile down the way.

Then two miles.

Three now. Maybe more? It's hard to judge without many landmarks.

It's fully dark now. I see every root that's about to catch me. I hear the wildlife skitter away from the sound of me crashing through the underbrush.

Apparently my sense of smell doesn't just apply to blood, as I catch a whiff of something distinct. Something familiar. A cheap and flowery perfume only Alex uses.

I stop moving, still down on all my limbs. I sniff the air. It's faint, but Alex was here. Which way is the wind blowing?

I take a second to orient myself. The sound of the wind through the leaves is the only thing that makes a sound. That is until I hear a noise I'm all too familiar with by now. A distant yelp of pain. I start to move but stop myself. It's pitch black out. Someone's gotten themselves hurt, and it could be Alex. I can't risk losing control around them. I also can't let them sit here on their own.

"Teratranza, what should I do?" I ask. The slight whimpers almost echo in my ears. All my senses must be as inhuman as I am.

"Thou now hast a heart. Thou must decide for thyself what that means and what to do with it." As she says it, the answer is clear. I have to follow my heart. If there's even a chance that's Alex, I have to get to them. I have to trust that I won't hurt them further.

I bring myself lower to the ground and begin to slink my way towards the scent and the noise. After a few minutes of slow, silent travel, I peek out of a bush to see a figure walking with a limp away from my direction.

I recognize them instantly. It's unmistakably Alex. With each step, they seem to wince in pain. What happened? I don't smell any blood, thank goodness. A sprain maybe? Tripped and fell? Except my questions die as I see an even more pressing concern.

There's a bear. A grizzly I think, and it's approaching Alex. I know bears mostly act out of curiosity around humans, but I also know that they're opportunistic hunters. Like me. This feels familiar. I recognize this. It wants Alex. This bear is moving ever so quietly through the trees for something of its size. Stalking. It's headed straight for Alex.

Not on my watch.

Alex has always been my guardian angel. Now it's time for me to be their guardian monster.

Chapter 13

HUNT

I charge just as the bear does. It's remarkably fast for something of its size but I reach Alex first. I pick them up with all four arms and shove them away from me, towards some bushes.

Profanities litter the air as I whirl around in time for the bear to be on top of me. I'm hunched down in a feral stance as it stands on its hide legs at its full height. It brings down its claw in a sharp rake across one of my forearms. Instantly it draws blood.

In spite of the bear's strength, the wound is more shallow than it should be, and the pain feels so dull. The force of a bear striking me should put me on my fucking ass, but as I'm still standing there, bracing myself against this animal.

There it is though: The dangerous scent of blood. Sweet, pure, delicious blood. I know it's my own. Practically, I know that, but that doesnt stop the Maw from groaning in hunger and my mouth beginning to salivate. Nor does it stop the rush of adrenaline that seeps through me.

"What in the fuck?!" I hear from behind me. Alex must be okay from that toss. Thank goodness.

"Stay away!" I growl at them. It comes out much more unhinged and aggressive than I intended, as the bear bites down hard on my upheld arms.

I feel the bones in one of my arms shatter. I can barely feel it though. I can't help the tone I just took with Alex as I feel the blood taking its hold of me.

I need Alex to stay away from me right now. I know for a fact that I'm more of a danger to them than the bear right now.

I catch the bear's paws with three out of four arms and shove them back with everything I've got. This bear must weigh at least five hundred some odd pounds, but three arms and supernatural, blood-rage fueled muscles are just enough to make it release my arm and stumble back a step or two.

It lands on all fours and then roars angrily back at me. I roar back, in unison with the Maw. It and I are all but the same now. I not only feel it but feel connected to it. Its want to feed one with my own. With one arm hanging limply at my side, the sounds the bear and I make echo through the forest as we throw ourselves at each other again.

The bear stands again and drags its claws across me faster than I ever expected something that big to move. I let the claws hit my shoulders as I use my own to swipe back at the bear. It has so much fat and fur covering its muscles that any cuts I do make are superficial at best.

I open my mouth wide and bite it's foreleg. I dig in deep and that seems to get its attention. The blood doesn't taste nearly as sweet as it normally does, but still tastes hardy like a steak and I can work with that.

The bear takes the opportunity to try and bite my neck itself. I swing an arm up, hand flexed, claws outstretched and land clean across its face. Their eye is not covered in fat or fur and comes right out of its socket. I rip my neck back taking a chunk of the bear's fur and meat with me. I spit the furry mess to the ground as the bear yowls in pain and shakes its head, turning the injury away from me.

My arm feels so numb from the exchanged blows as blood continues to flow from the bite and continues to pool on the forest floor. As it's smell and taste continues to fuel my rampage.

I wail a hollow and shrill noise as I raise to my full height. The bear actually seems to hesitate, like they didn't expect such resistance. It takes a step back.

I don't hesitate or step back. I charge at the beast, tearing my way across the ground unevenly with all my functioning limbs.

Before they can move, I pounce at them. The bear rises to meet me and we tumble backwards hitting the ground hard. It's a flurry of teeth and claws. I'm tough now, but I'm losing a lot of blood. Adrenaline can only take me so far, but the bear didn't expect such a hard fight. It expected easy, injured prey, and I guarantee it didn't expect to get hurt like it did.

We keep fighting to be on top of the other as we rip into each other. When it has me under it finally, it snaps at my shoulder and bites down with all the force expected out of a cornered animal. That hurts. That I feel, but I wont get a better shot. I take all three functioning sets of claws and begin repeatedly ripping into the bear's underbelly.

It tries to shake its head back and forth to shred my shoulder, but the force of the bite begins to lessen. I've hit organs now. I know the feel as well as I know the taste. I don't stop. I keep shredding its insides until it falls limp on me. Dead or dying at least.

I roll it off me with what strength I have left. I drag myself to my knees and sit there, huffing as I try to catch my breath. My visions are blurry and tinged with red. My broken arm is completely numb. Intestines, blood, and meat cover the ground around me. I'm disoriented, but I feel it in me, like an impulse. An urge.

FEED.

I throw myself at the bear's open belly and begin to tear in, using my functioning arms to tear the wound open wider. To get to the blood and muscles and guts and delicious food.

My arm starts to gain feeling back and I immediately use them to begin shoveling food into my mouths.

The bear's meat is dense but not filling. I need more.

I crack open its ribs and rip out its heart with my teeth. I throw my head back, open wider than I ever thought possible and swallow the entire thing, my throat bulging unnaturally as it goes down.

I can feel my skin knitting back together with a hiss being released into the air from my wounds. It burns. It burns so good. The impulse does not lessen.

MORE.

The bear quickly turns into a shell of itself. A hollow cavity is all that faces me. I feel fully recovered and fully enamored by the meal.

MORE! MORE! MORE!

Then I hear it: a crack. A tree branch snapping. I raise my head and spin it around to look over my shoulder. A figure stands, leaning against a tree. My vision is so filled with red it's nothing but a silhouette. I recognize what it is though. More food.

I charge at the figure, closing in fast. It raises its arms to shield itself, but I grab them and pull them aside, not letting go. I grab it's throat and raise my final arm, poised to strike. I start to bring it down towards the things chest when I hear a choked noise escape its lips.

"Dax!" Says the thing in my grasp. Dax?

I pause mid swing, uncertainty breaking through my hazy state. Who is... wait. That's me? That's me! Only one person calls me Dax though? That can't- oh god!

I realize with a start as to who I must be gripping like a ragdoll. I release the figure and they fall to the ground. I grab my head by the horns and begin to shake my head back and forth, covering my eyes.

No no no!

Calm down! Calm down! I can't! I can't!

Another voice fills the air now. One I recognize almost as quickly as I recognized the other. Teratranza utters one word.

"Calm."

As if a spell were spoken into existence, and for all I know, one just was, the red begins to slowly fade from the black behind my closed eyes. I stop thrashing back and forth and slowly open and uncover my eyes, blinking a few times and still gripping my horns for dear life.

"Alex?" I ask, uncertain of myself. I look in their direction as they slowly come into focus.

They're on their hands and knees. Coughing. A bruise is already forming around their neck. They look up, one eye closed in strain.

"Yeah, it's me." They choke out.

For a second we both just look at each other in the moonlight. For me it's like seeing them basking in the sun.

I can't imagine what they must see when they look at me. Ripped up clothes covering a misshapen form of claws and teeth and utterly covered in blood. Are my eyes reflective like a cat's? Am I just a hulking freak of an animal to them? They just saw me fight an actual bear and not only win against it, but mutilate it. I must look hideous to them. But still, they called my name?

Alex starts to grin.

"And here I thought I could beat you to the cabin." They cough once more, some blood comes up with it this time.

I flinch away and cover my head with my arms, but nothing comes. No sudden bloodlust. No rush. Everything smells like blood right now but it smells... normal? Like how blood smelt before. Unremarkable and like pennies.

A few moments pass where I'm too scared to move. Scared of what I just did. Then I feel a hand gently place itself on one of my arms.

"You okay?" Alex asks.

"Am I okay? You almost died! Twice! First the bear, then me!" I sob. "How can you be concerned about me right now?" I shift my arms slightly and peek out at their face. It's remarkably beautiful in the light of the moon.

"Easily." They reply simply.

Alex's smile isn't their usual one, all cocky and self assured, but they're smiling nonetheless though. They look me in the eye. They take a step back, and extend a hand.

It's a ridiculous gesture. Their leg is obviously hurt. They couldn't possibly help my now massive self up. Despite all of that, I uncover my head and hesitantly reach out one of my hands before stopping short and pulling back.

"I'm covered in blood..." I mutter looking away in shame.

Alex makes another wincing noise as I hear them lower themselves to my level and I feel as they grab either side of my face. Alex gently makes me look at them. Makes me meet their gaze again.

"I don't care." They say before opening up their arms and leaning forward into me. A hug.

I'm covered in gore, they've seen what I look like now, and they've seen me desecrate and eat a grizzly. They're still giving me a hug.

I don't move to hug them back. My arms hang limply by my sides. A second passes where I can't tell what I'm feeling. Where I can't tell what to do next. Tears well up in my eyes.

Oh. Okay.

I begin to cry into their shoulders. I wrap them up in a massive hug as gently as I can, pulling them in as closely as I can without hurting them further.

We sit there like that for longer than it took to kill the bear. For longer than we've hugged before. Just sitting there. Together.

Chapter 14

ALEX

Alex is the first to speak.

"I like ribbon," they say softly, "it suits you."

I laugh at the absurdity of the statement in the midst of every other thing they could comment on. Of course they would notice that.

I pull away from them, one set of arms still hanging around their neck.

"Thanks," I chuckle, "you look stunning yourself." I say, embarrassed the second it leaves my mouth.

No. Following your heart, remember? These emotions aren't new. Alex laughs this time. A sudden burst of cheery warmth.

"I bet I look like shit right now. Thanks for the toss by the way. Almost twisted my other ankle." They state without a hint of actual displeasure in their voice.

I let my arms pull away from them, despite wanting to hold them for the rest of the night. "So you are hurt then? We should get you back to town. I can carry you?" I offer.

I could be mistaken but I swear there's a hint of blush to Alex's face when I say that. They look away from me.

"No. No going back there now." They declare.

The look on their face is hard to place as they turn back to me because it quickly changes to smiling again. I could have sworn they looked... Sad? Mournful? I've seen them upset and happy and mad even, but I don't think I've ever seen such a look of regret on their face. It makes my chest ache.

"Let's just get to the cabin, yeah? That was the plan." They say, almost pleading. There's a desperation in their voice. That scares me.

"Plan? What plan? You dropped all this on me out of nowhere! Why can't we just get you somewhere safe and assess the damage, Alex? Why go to the cabin in the first place?" I implore. The look of guilt now on their face is unmistakable.

"I'll explain when we get there. The cabin is the only place I'll feel safe right now, okay? Can we leave it at that?"

"No we cannot." Teratranza's voice sounds jarring in the middle of our conversation. Alex jumps and looks shocked at my abdomen.

"Thou Lamentable thing art as crooked as the Monstrous thing thou sees before thee. Speak the entirety of the truth or I shall know." She proclaims.

I look down, shocked as well now. She's accusing Alex of lying? Wait, Alex did mention hiding something from me, but I thought it was just their illness?

I look back up at them and see terror on their face. Oh god, Teratranza was a step too far for them to handle! Alex could accept me but they don't know about Teratranza! I start to form an apology and excuses in my head before Alex finally speaks.

"F-fine." Alex says falteringly. Alex begins to fidget and look uncomfortable. What I mistook for terror seems to be something closer to trepidation.

"The cabin belonged to a relative of mine. I figure you'll be safe from the law and I'll be safe from my parents." They say slowly, gauging my reaction.

They weren't scared of Teratranza then, but at being called out. There's a lot of information there, I don't know what to ask first. I sit there mouth agape like an idiot.

"See? That was not so hard! Thou may now proceed to the cabin at thy leisure." Alex continues to stare at the spot on my stomach where the demon speaks through before just sighing, exasperated.

"I'll explain as we go, but maybe you go first with the explanations?" Alex says, reaching for their discarded backpack that must've fallen off when I tossed them aside.

They're struggling to stand, however, so I quickly stand and begin to support them on their way up.

"I have questions too.how about we take turns?" I quite literally sweep Alex off their feet, bag in tow. I don't want them hurting their leg any further. I can see a bit of purple peeking out between their socks and pant leg.

Alex's face definitely reddens this time. They hug their bag tightly in their arms "S-sure. Can I ask first?" They mumble.

"The stage is yours." I say announce dramatically. This gets their cocky smile back. It's refreshing to see after the events of the last twelve or so hours.

"Alright then, lets start with 'What the fuck!?'" They shout, gesturing at me. I can't help but let a small laugh leak out.

"That's, uh, a long story. Mind narrowing the question down?" I ask.

"Sure, but that counts as your question then, just so you know." Alex says with a crooked grin. "How about... who's that other voice?"

"I am Domina Mutationis!" Interjects the demon yet again. "Or the Lady of Change, but one so close to my Monstrous thing may call me by my name: Teratranza."

"She's the demon I made a deal with. For... well, all this." I try to gesture to myself while holding Alex steady. Alex, for their part, doesn't widen their eyes or drop their jaw. They jus nod along, thoughtfully.

"Makes sense." They state. "What?" I ask, taken aback.

"You made a deal with a demon. Makes sense. Though I'm still trying to figure out what you asked for." Alex declares, as if demonic deals are a common occurrence.

"Is that your next question?" I inquire, allowing their declaration earlier about my first question to be true. I can never say no to them.

"Nope. My next question is how fast can you run carrying me? I'd rather get moving soon." They say with slight urgency, before pausing and glancing towards the Maw. "My parents will be looking for me soon."

Teratranza is keeping them honest. That's good for me. I won't hide anything either. No more hiding. Not from Alex.

"Let's find out." I say, cradling Alex in my arms, bracing them. I take a second to kick and stretch my legs, orient myself towards the cabin's direction, and then bolt.

I'm not as fast as before when I was on all six limbs, but it's like sticking my head out the window of a moving vehicle as the wind races by me. I'm sprinting as fast as I can manage without shaking Alex too much. For their part, Alex looks astonished. Their hearty cheer echoes through the woods.

"Fuck yeah!" They exclaim, with the yeah extending several seconds.

"My turn," I start, smiling and reveling in the feeling of this speed, " why are your parents after you this time?"

"What!?" Alex shouts, looking up at me. I start to restate my question a bit louder, but Alex cuts me off. "I'm sorry! I can't hear you at all!"

Damn. I was hoping to interrogate them now but I guess I'll just have time to organize my thoughts.

I leap, jump and tear my way through the forest floor, spotting and avoiding every root and bramble I could trip on.

I feel energized. I feel alive! That meal has me feeling a hundred percent!

I can't help but wonder if that will trigger a change though. I doubt it. It seemed to progress faster the second time so I assume it'll be even faster on the third go around.

Besides that theory, Teratranza strikes me as gluttonous yes, but she also strikes me as a picky eater.

It takes us just an hour or two to get there with the speed at which I can effectively move through the forest. As soon as the cabin is in sight I begin to slow down. I don't even feel that winded. This new body is ridiculous. I can only imagine what a third change will gift me with. 'My final blooming' Teratranza called it.

"Uh.. you can put me down now. I think I can walk this little bit." Alex mumbles uncertainly. The same flushed expression sits on their face. I could grow very used to that look. That is, if I wasn't feeling equally as flustered myself.

"Sure. Is this okay?" I manage as I set them down, and support their weight as they begin to take steps forward.

"Yeah, just give me a second." Alex says.

We reach the door and Alex begins rummaging through the bag they've been holding. "Better not have fallen out... There it is!" Alex pulls out something small and metallic.

"What do you have there?" I inquire.

"The key." Alex says, voice neutral. They look back at me with something like embarrassment on their face before unlocking the door. "I still can't believe you relock the locks you pick."

"I've gotta cover my tracks, but hey, don't distract me. Why do you have a key to this place?" I demand.

"Is that your question?" Alex asks with what I can tell is a forced grin. I find myself getting a little frustrated with their insistence on taking nothing seriously. It never has before, but this matters to me.

"I need to know why you needed to come here and how you knew about it in the first place, so yes, 'why the key' is my question." I assert. Alex looks away as they twist the key in the knob. The door opens with a slow creaking.

"It was my grandparent's place. I took the key from my parents when I... left this time. I said I had to grab some stuff, remember?" Alex says as they limp in. They pull out a flashlight and shine it into the dark of the cabin.

I briefly shield my eyes before Alex clicks something on the flashlight and it dims. "Sorry! I didn't know- your eyes I mean-" Alex says blurt out, stumbling over themselves. "It's fine." I moan, eyes adjusting slowly to the less intense light.

I walk in after Alex as they shuffle with purpose towards the back room and sit down at what could be a kitchen table if this place wasn't so decrepit.

I pull out a chair opposite them before thinking better of the rotted wood. I instead move the chair aside and sit cross legged on the ground across from Alex. Our eyes are still about the same level.

Alex sets the flashlight on the table facing up, gently lightening the room enough so they can presumably see me better.

"My turn." Alex begins. "Is this body what you asked for? I knew you weren't trans too but I didn't quite expect everything I'm seeing. No offence intended of course, you look happier already!" The words hit me like a slap in the face.

"How'd you know for sure?" I demand. Alex shrugs.

"Same things I've seen in myself. Our similarities are a lot more than just music taste. I wasn't going to pressure you though." Alex explains.

After a minute or two of silence, trying to think about how to explain it, I finally speak. "It's not just that I'm trans. I'm not even human. I've always felt it deep in my bones in a way I'll never be able to articulate." I raise a hand up in front of me like I'm studying my nails. "I lacked claws, fangs, and more in the same way I lacked a more feminine body. I'm a Monster. Or something like that at least. I just look the part a little better now." Alex doesn't hesitate to ask their next question.

"Are you happy?" They ask.

"I... I think I am. I'm not where I want to be, but I'm better. So much better now. You know?" I reply, briefly forgetting the turns in our little question game.

"I think I do." Alex says with a genuine smile.

Alex hasn't been on hormones that long in the grand scheme of things, just since they turned eighteen and their parents couldn't stop them anymore, but Alex has been living as their true self for a majority of the time I've known them. Five whole years of being out. Of knowing who you are and expressing it more and more each day. I'm fairly sure that at this exact moment, Alex really does understand. Someone actually understands.

I begin to tear up in joy for the second time today. I wipe my eyes. My joy turns slowly to dread, however, as I steel myself for the answer to my next question.

"You're sick. Aren't you? What is it?" I say with as much seriousness and gentleness as I can muster. I can't have their usual jokes and games as comforting as they are. I need to know.

They don't meet my gaze. They just look down at their hands on the table as they fidget like crazy.

"Lung cancer." They finally admit. That vise-like grip around my heart returns with a vengeance. A clutching ache deep in my chest.

"I always told you to stop smoking..." Is all I can manage to say.

It's stupid and besides the point but it's all I can think of. Alex for their part chuckles a little.

"It wasn't the cigarettes." They state matter of factly.

"What do you mean?" I ask.

"It's my turn to ask a question." Alex deflects.

"Bullshit. How long then? How long do you have? Can we treat it? I can find a way to pay for any treatments you need!" I babble. Alex finally meets my gaze.

"It wasn't the cigarettes. It was my price to pay for the deal I made with my own demon. It can't be treated and I don't have long." Alex responds calmly. They pull something from their bag and place it on the table. "To put it into perspective, I went and grabbed both the key and this from my parents. To go out on my own terms."

It's a handgun. I don't know what kind but I always knew Alex's dad owned one. He threatened them with it enough times that I had to know. I go dead still.

Alex came here to die.

Chapter 15

CLARITY

"Why'd you call me here to begin with!?" I say, desperate anger filling my voice. My claws all dig into the wood floor. "How could you not tell me? What deal was worth dying for?" I shout at them.

I'm angry and upset but most of all feeling betrayed. My best friend was planning on leaving me tonight. I saw the signs but I couldn't have known that they were dying until this afternoon. That they were suffering so much that they were deciding to die.

Alex just sighs.

"You deserve the full story." They respond softly. I'm damned near hyperventilating and I can feel myself tearing up again. I wait for them to continue, but they don't.

"Well?! Then give me the full story!" I yell at them.

I only relent when I see them tearing up as well. I don't think I've ever seen Alex cry since we were kids. It never even occurred to me that they still could.

"I'm sorry, okay? Just... Just give me a second." They wipe their own tears away and I can't help but reach out a long arm across the table and set a hand on their shoulder.

"I'm sorry for yelling. You just dropped a lot on me. Please take your time. You know I care about you." I comfort them, saying whatever comes to mind the second it does. Who cares if It's embarrassing to say how much I care about them, they deserve to hear it and didn't deserve me taking my frustration out on them.

They recover after a few more seconds, enough to begin talking at least. I go to move my hand back, but Alex puts their hands across their chest onto my hand, keeping it there.

"You know I came out to my parents at thirteen. You know that didn't go well, right? My dad still calls me a 'freak of nature' and says I'm 'sinning by existing'. My mom always took a more neutral response. Saying 'God still loves you' and 'I just don't understand'. That didn't stop any of how my father treated me though." Alex pauses to take a shaky breath. They squeeze my hand. I can tell this is uncomfortable for them to speak about. I immediately feel worse for forcing the issue, but I listen intently to what they have to say.

"I couldn't take it anymore. I couldn't take the constant invalidation, threats, and pain they caused me. So... I tried to kill myself after three months of that treatment." This hits me hard. The realization that this isn't the first time Alex has tried to take their life. That vice around my heart twists.

"I couldn't picture myself ever being happy or loved. Or even surviving what was being done to me. I knew my grandparents lived here in the woods when they were young, before the town was what it really was today. So I ran away, came here, and then stabbed myself. Stuck a knife right into my stomach. I had no idea what I was doing. It hurt. It hurt more than anything I had ever physically experienced had hurt before. I pulled the knife out and fell to my hands and knees." As Alex lets go of my hand, I take my hand back and find myself beginning to pick at the floor nervously with my claws. The wood gives way easily. Alex pauses their story to pull out something else from their bag. This I recognize instantly.

The journal.

They toss it into the table with which shakes the gun and knocks the flashlight over. They don't bother picking it up.

"The journal was here though, sitting on that shelf." They point past me towards the room by the entrance. "As soon as my vision began to fade, I swear I saw that book open up and the temperature just dropped noticeably. Much more so than just the feeling of dying. I could see the frost forming on everything around me. When I finally collapsed and faded, I thought the pain would stop, but it continued. I found myself floating in an empty black space filled with stars and the pain in my gut continued to burn." I recognize Alex's description mirroring my own summoning, and find myself horrified by what they went through for theirs.

"A demon was summoned then? By your… attempt?" I ask incredulously.

"Turns out, yeah. Pretty shit requirements for a ritual, right? I couldn't see him, and the pain made it hard to focus on his words. He spoke in a language I couldn't place, but I heard an echo in my head, like a translation of his words. That echo was in Spanish. He seemed to know I'd simply just understand whatever he said as he spoke into my mind. 'Yo soy Alegría y dolor.' I am Joy and Pain. He didn't give me a name, but he made me an offer. 'Vida de alegría, a cambio de muerte de dolor?' With it being projected into my mind, I understood perfectly what he meant despite the pain taking my focus from me." Alex pauses here, like they're bracing themselves for what they are about to say.

"He would give me one of the things I felt I was missing from my life. He would give me happiness, but the second I experience the other thing I was missing, I would begin to die." Alex looks at me then, with a solemn smile and it clicks with me.

"Love." I mutter. "You'd begin to die the second you experience love."

"It seems that way..." Alex trails off, like they're flashing back to that day. "I was in so much pain. The knife wound hurt, yeah, but more so it hurt knowing I would never experience the love and happiness others did on my own. So when that offer was made, I accepted. I woke up the next day, with a bloody knife in my hand and a scar on my stomach." Alex lifts their shirt with one hand just enough to show the scar. A thin horizontal slash above their belly button. They drop the shirt and plop their hands back down on the table. I can tell this has drained them, but they continue to speak in spite of that.

"I wandered back through the woods and... well I ran into you." Alex seems nervous now.

Fidgeting and looking anywhere but at my face.

I remember that day. The day we really became friends. We had both run away at the same time and were wandering through the woods towards our respective homes. We ran into each other and spent the whole day talking and getting to know each other on our way back to town. We'd known each other beforehand but we clicked almost instantly that day.

"What are you saying? I say slowly, expressing my confusion.

Alex weakly laughs which turns into a coughing fit. I reach out but they hold up a hand. After a little longer than I'm comfortable with, they pull their fist away from their mouth and it's covered in blood where their mouth was. I still have no reaction to the sight or smell of the blood though. Thank you, Teratranza, so much for that. She does not respond.

"You still don't get it?" Asks Alex with a smile, blood leaking from the sides of their mouth. "I asked for happiness and we became friends. My parents were the same after that.

Nothing else changed except for us, and I need you to know that you made me so happy. I fought for who I was and I had you by my side supporting me. I had you to laugh with, someone who shared my interests and most of all just someone who made me smile all the time. All the demon had to do to make me happy was introduce us further, Dax. You've made me so happy over the years that I..." Alex holds out their hand for me. I can't believe what they're saying but I reach out a hand and place it on theirs, regardless of my bewilderment. "...That I fell in love with you, Dax." If their words to me before were a slap in the face, this was like skydiving without a parachute. Alex feels the same way I do.

"I realized about a year ago. But nothing changed. I didn't start to die. I didn't get sick. So I knew you didn't feel the same and I didn't act on it. I was happy with you. With whatever form that took, but I saw the way you looked at me on my birthday. I felt my heart skip a beat and a pulse through my whole body. I knew you wanted to kiss me in that moment." They look at me and their face goes scarlet. "Thats the moment I knew you loved me too."

No. No it can't be like this.

"I... I killed you. It's my fault then that you're dying." Alex winces and I realize I am squeezing their hand, claws digging in slightly. I try to pull my hand away in horror but Alex clasps their other hand on mine, keeping it there and squeezing back.

"I killed myself. Not you. Years ago. I've been living on borrowed time. A ghost of myself. My death was always going to be painful. The demon just made sure it could harvest my pain. The happier the life, the worse the pain of my death. I suppose emotional pain counts to a demon." Alex mutters that last part.

"But when I realized I was dying, and I saw you going down the same road I did, I decided to do something for you." Alex exclaims, perking up slightly. "Over the years, I'd researched and translated as much of the book here as I could without my parents finding out. They hated our grandparents for 'defying god'. I only ever found out three things though. The first being that the demon I met doesn't have a name beyond a title: El Agridulce Segador. The Bittersweet Reaper. Second, that my family has a long history of working with demons and monsters. The book was put together over years and generations. Finally, I learned that you can only make a deal with one demon at a time. Something about your soul only being able to handle the pull of one demon at a time without being ripped out of you. I couldn't make a deal to help you, or to make you happy after I was gone. So I did the next best thing I could think of."

"You told me where to find the book then. Why not give it to me in the first place? Explain any of what was going on?" I question.

"My parents." Alex says with contempt. They found out I'd been going here and hid the key from me. It took me forever to find it again and I knew you could pick locks and had a fascination with the occult. So I thought you could figure something out. Make your own happiness. I put the tools for it in your hands because I didn't want to influence what you would do. I didn't want you making a deal to keep me alive, I wanted you to make yourself happy. Now please. Tell me about your happiness. Tell me about the deal you made?"

I hesitate. I promised myself I'd be honest but just how much do I share. It feels like Alex hid so much from me, but it also feels like they just laid bare their very heart and soul to me just now.

"Go on then, Monstrous Thing, tell them of our pact. This has proven most interesting." Teratranza commands, amusement in her voice. I forget sometimes that she's always there. The levity she speaks with aggravates me for a moment before I can gather myself and answer Alex's plea.

"I... I summoned Teratranza. Teratranza is the 'Eater of the Ancient' and creator of the new. She is change itself. So I gave my old body and self for my new one." I start. "I'm still me though! Just... more, you know?" They nod along and are looking at me expectantly. Fuck it, hear goes nothing. "My changes still needed fuel though. I had to feed both Teratranza and myself. And Teratranza has a particular appetite that, uh, well…" I trail off, finding that admitting to being a murderer is quite hard.

"So that's why Justin and Amanda are dead then? You ate them?" Alex says curiously. I look up at them, aghast. "What? You can't hide anything from me. Never have been able to. I went back for the hoodie you left at the creek after I dropped you off at home, only to find what was left of Justin. As for Amanda... Well, you kinda gave me that evidence." They pick up and shake the flashlight in their hand. I only then realize that it's the same as Amanda's. Some of the blood on it isn't the fresh red blood I got on Alex's hands. Some of it is dried and brown. It's not like Amanda's flashlight, it is Amanda's.

"You knew? You knew this whole time that I've killed someone?" I beg as conflicted feelings build in my gut. One thing is certain though: Alex really didn't turn me in for murder. Which means Alex must be telling the truth about how they feel about me. Why else would they keep my secret? I don't think I know how to process this rush of feelings that flood through me.

"Yeah, I knew. I had my suspicions when I found the blood stained hoodie and scene you left behind that you made a deal with something. When you were rapidly getting sick, I'll admit I was uncertain and concerned for you, but what confirmed both that you made a pact and that you had killed Justin was when the next day you were suddenly able to walk on your own again, were covering everything up, and rumors about Justin never making it home started to circulate the school." Alex pauses their explanation for a second, seeming to think about what they are about to say. "I understand Justin. If you had to kill then he was target number one for sure, but why Amanda? I thought she liked you. I thought that maybe she could... I don't know, make you happy after I left." They look a little despondent at this last part, as Amanda and I getting together would have consoled them in their last moments.

"You idiot," I say as I reach out and cup their face with two hands. "She may have been into me, which took me by quite the surprise, trust me," I divulge, which makes Alex chuckle just a little through the confused expression on their face, "but I only ever wanted you. Only you."

I can't help but stare at their lips now. Would they let me... no, not like this. Not as the monster I am. Maybe before, but I missed my chance. "She came onto me and found out how I looked. She started freaking out and attacked me when someone," I glare down at the Maw, "told her I killed her twin."

"You're looking at me like that again." Is all Alex says, ignoring the fact that I just confessed to two murders, before leaping out of my hands and over the table at me. I flinch, not knowing what's coming next.

When their lips touch mine, I swear it feels like a dream. It's a dream I've had many times before and it feels so unreal, like I'm floating again in Teratranza's strange void. But, fuck, does it also feels so good. Their arms are wrapped around my neck and I kiss them back, carefully resisting the urge to bite their lip. While it would still feel hot as hell, it'd be a lot more deadly now to do so.

The passion they meet me with feels so 'Alex'. Doing everything with their full self. Never holding back. Well, except they have been holding back from doing exactly this it seems. There's a hunger in them that I recognize all too well. A desire. For a second, I'm lost in the moment as all four of my hands trace their face and body.

I have to pull back first, breathless and as close to ripping into them as I am to ripping their clothes off. This feels dangerous, but I can't help but love it. Love them. Alex pants for a good while, not taking their eyes off me and grinning like an idiot.

"Finally," they say, "I've been waiting for that for a long time."

"What now?" I ask. I'm a monster and Alex is dying, but we finally have each other. What comes after this?

"Dax?" Alex starts, still breathless.

"Yeah?" I answer. At this moment, I'd do anything for them. Alex leans up to my ear and whispers, "I want you to eat me."

Chapter 16

DEVOUR

I jump backwards out of Alex's arms, knocking over the chair next to me as I stand, startled and confused. I must've heard them wrong. Alex almost falls off the table but manages to catch themself.

"Dax... please." Alex begs. It's only now their request fully sinks in.

"How could you possibly ask that of me? You kiss me, then ask me to kill you? What's wrong with you?!" I raise my voice, anger boiling up as I speak. I don't want to yell at them again, but I don't know how else to react to being begged to kill the love of your life.

"A lot of things are wrong with me." Alex answers sarcastically, but I know them well enough to tell they're masking how they really feel right now. "Mostly the fact that I'm dying. Soon. The plan was always to go out on my own terms." They move to sit up on the table, facing me, and gesture at the gun that got kicked aside in our moment of passion. "That hasn't changed, but you have. You've changed things. You said it yourself that you need to feed to change and that you don't quite feel like your full self but that you're getting closer. You need to eat more, right? And I'm already dead." Alex reaches for me but I take a step back, scared of what I'll do to them if I touch them. Like I'm already guaranteed to end them if we touch. "Please let it be you."

I'm shaking now. Part of me was so caught up in the moment that my visions of the future for us weren't so short lived. Reality kicks in with their words. The urge I had to tear into them moments previous. The knowledge that I need to eat someone I envy. Or does any strong emotion work? If envy gave me all of this, what more could love give me. Fuel me. My final bloom. The fact that Alex is dying anyway...

"No!" I shout! "I can't! I don't ever want to hurt you." I declare, mostly to myself.

"I'm sorry Dax, but you kind of already did" Alex rubs their throat, which is very much bruising from my grip on them earlier.

"T-that was an accident... I'd never willingly hurt you. It's blood. It.. it makes me go crazy now. Feral. I have a need for it. An urge." I explain desperately as guilt and regret overtake my anger.

"I know it was an accident." They stand and step closer, and this time I let them. "I'm fairly certain though, that the only reason I'm not torn limb from limb right now is because your demon took pity on me. It's not your fault, but it is your responsibility. You have an urge to consume. You chose this. Let me choose for myself now. Let me feed you."

"If Teratranza can stop me from hurting you then we're fine! We have time! I'll complete my deal and make another to save you!" I bargain.

"It won't last, my poor lovers." announces Teratranza. "I need fuel to act. That bear's body was enough to heal thee, and its soul was enough for me to stop thy bloodlust for some time, but there are not enough souls within these woods nor this town to save the life of this one. A deal is a deal, always." I look between the Maw and Alex in horror. Alex seems to nod along as if they expected as much.

"Isn't there anything we can do?" I plead to Teratranza and Alex.

"What would you do, Monstrous thing? Kill every living soul you find to stave off thy truest hungers?"

"Yes!" I say with no hesitation. "For Alex I would!" I turn to leave but Alex grasps one of my wrists with both hands and since I don't want to hurt them by ripping it out of their grip, I pause.

"Dax, please listen. I'm going to die. We can't stop that. You need another victim, so why not a willing one?" I turn to face them again and they take two of my hands in theirs, gently. "Soon enough her spell will wear off, right? Assuming I don't end it now, you'd have to avoid me coughing up blood, or risk killing me as brutally as you did the bear. You can make this as painless as possible. That demon's already gonna get all my emotional baggage and pain when I die. No reason to let it harvest my physical pain too."

"I don't want to lose you. We can still spend what time we have together. Besides, how could I even kill you painlessly? These teeth aren't exactly for show." I rebuke.

"This is gonna sound weird, but you can fit a whole body in there right?" Alex asks, looking at the Maw. I nod slowly, not following. "Why not an intact one? Instead of ripping me to pieces, let me crawl in. Swallow me whole. No biting. Well, maybe a little." Alex winks at me, but I don't fluster for once. What they're suggesting is so absurd. I'm not even questioning whether or not it's possible, but why the hell would Alex want this? Alex says they love me but to die at my hand? To be consumed by me?

"Assuming that's even possible," I take my hands out of theirs and wrap all four arms around myself in a tight hug. I look away, unable to meet their gaze. "Why? Tell me the truth. Why are you so desperate to die at my hand? Being devoured hasn't exactly been pleasant for anyone as far as I'm aware. You do realize that right?" Out of the corner of my eyes, I can see Alex reach for me before pausing. They look away from me themselves, before looking back at me and I can't help but look back at them. They just pull me in, everything about them.

"I... I see them in you. Justin and Amanda. Their features. It's like they're getting to stay with you, but I'm not. It's unfair. I want to stay. I don't want to die." Alex begins to tear up but doesn't look away from me. "I want to stay here with you. I want to be with you. I want to always be close to you. If my only option for that is to become a part of you, then so be it. I'll do so gladly." Alex's tears are freely flowing down their face. I lift a hand to wipe the tears away from their cheek but they tackle hug me. If I wasn't as strong as I am now, I'd be on my ass.

Alex squeezes me, burying their face into my chest, making me a little self conscious, but more than that, it makes me feel their pain all the more and I just want to comfort them. I want us to stay together. I want them to live. I want them to be happy.

It's too late though. I can smell their blood again. The spell is fading and a choice has to be made. Fast.

"Will you be happy?" I say, breaking through the noise of their sobs. It takes them a second to respond, but through the sniffles they mutter, "Happier than I've ever been." They look up at me, pleading. They look so desperate. So sad. So determined. Who am I to deny my love's dying wish?

"...Okay." I mutter.

"What?" Alex asks in disbelief, raising an arm to wipe their face.

"I... I'll do it. If it's what you really want, and if there's nothing that can change your mind, I'll do it." Alex seems to slowly register what I said. A weak smile begins to appear on their face. Their eyebrows still knit together in distress.

"Dax, do you really mean it?" Alex asks with such sincerity, it makes me want to hold them here forever. It makes me want to dig my claws in deep and never let go. It makes me want to... fucking hell... I want to eat them. It's not just the bloodlust, I can tell. I want them to be a part of me as much as they want the same. I want us to be inseparable. My desire has always been all consuming, but now consumption and desire are nearly one in the same.

I don't know how much longer I can hold back. My tail is whipping back and forth now, swishing across the floor, raising dust. I can feel my body preparing to feast. My body tensing, my claws digging into my own arms, my jaw and Maw beginning to gnash slightly. My senses are sharpening. The blood on Alex's lips is so tempting. but I can't risk another kiss. Not like this.

That was it. Our one and only. I'll remember it forever.

"Dax. I can tell you're holding back. "Alex notes with a softness in their voice. "You don't have to anymore."

I catch myself drooling a little and wipe it from my face. I look Alex in the eyes once more and just nod. No more holding back. No more hiding.

I step back and Alex lets me free from their embrace. I miss it already.

I get down on one knee, and brace myself with my arms as I prepare to lean back and open the Maw.

"Alex?" I get their attention. "Yeah?" They answer.

"I'm going to miss you." I say with guilt filling my voice. Alex gets down on their knees now in front of me.

"I'm not going anywhere." Alex promises with a soft grin.

"I love you." I choke out through my tightening throat as I lean back, opening the Maw as wide as I can, getting my last glimpse of Alex.

"I love you, too." Alex says with certainty.

I can no longer see them, but I can feel them as they place their hand on my Maw's outstretched tongue. Their hands are so warm and a shiver runs through them as they touch me.

My spine is bent so far backwards, it should be snapped in two. The Maw is open wider than ever before and stays that way. Long, drawn out, gentle breaths I never noticed before flow from my Maw as I myself breathe. Alex gently slides their hand up along the tongue as they place their other hand on it as well.

They're moving so slowly and the subtle taste of their skin is already divine as is. I want more. I want to bite into them. I want to feel their blood splatter against the inside of the Maw.

I...

I need to calm down. This isn't for me. It's for Alex. 'But can't it be both?' A part of me argues.

"You ready?" Asks Alex suddenly, sounding nervous. Are they having second thoughts? "No. Are you?" I manage through my growing desire. They manage a soft laugh.

"No." They say as they continue anyway.

They begin to crawl forward, and I feel everything. As they shift themselves and force their way into me, I can't help but feel a rush. Excitement. An eager craving for them. They feel so good inside of me.

It's a tight fit. Their arms reach back into nothingness as their head and shoulders begin to pass by the sharp teeth of my Maw. Some of the sharp edges scrape against their clothes and then skin as they crawl their way further. The small amount of blood that flows onto my tongue is like ambrosia or even ichor. The food and blood of the Greek deities themselves. The sweetest blood I've ever tasted.

I let out a moan of sheer delight as Alex lets out a soft muffled cry of pain . My teeth have started to sink into them on impulse. I pull myself back further to remove my fangs from their back and give them some breathing room.

"Sorry…" I mutter through the haze of desire flooding my body. They continue moving in, and as soon as their chest is fully inside me, I can feel myself growing impatient. I'm digging my claws into my palms, drawing blood, trying to hold myself back from biting them in half.

It's too much, I can't handle it. I need Alex. I need them inside me. I need them as part of me. I need them. I need them!

My Maws tongue stretches out from under them, grabbing them between the legs, prompting a yelp from Alex, as my arms all grip their legs and begin to push them inwards. There's some shocked sounding muffled words I can't quite make out, but they aren't struggling at all. With that being the case, their shock is not my focus at the moment. My focus is devouring them. Devouring Alex whole.

They wanted this. They asked for this. Now I want it too. So badly. Only their legs are sticking out of me now and I could so easily crunch them. I don't do it though. Instead, I wrap my long tongue around their left leg and just pull them into me. I can't tell if they're struggling or not anymore as there's not enough of them left to show it. That doesn't matter much anymore though as in a matter of seconds, the last of Alex disappears behind the teeth of my Maw as it slams shut. My upper body shifts forward violently and I catch myself on the ground with all four arms.

It's still and silent in the cabin. I'm alone.

"That one was quite the interesting creature." Teratranza pipes up. I go to slowly stand in a daze, before I catch a glimpse of something on the ground. Something metal and small. I pick it up. It's Alex's necklace. The counterpart to mine. A skeleton with their arms crossed.

Alex is gone now. I'm alone. In spite of the sheer exaltation I felt moments ago, I find that the rapture in my blood rapidly fades. I ate the person I loved. I feel more numb and hurt than I ever did before I began all this.

There's a part of me, though, that still feels such pleasure from what just happened. It's intoxicating. Alex was intoxicating. Now, soon, they'll be a part of me.

"Art thou... well? Twas their decision and thy desire. It was always going to end up this way, was it not?" Teratranza poses the question to me as if she herself is unsure. Or maybe she's just concerned about my wellbeing.

I slowly put on the necklace. I open the coffin on my necklace and slip their skeleton inside it. I shift the coffin closed. A matching set. Together forever.

"I was always going to end this way, yeah, you're probably right." I admit numbly. "You get the soul, I get the body. That's how it works right?".

"Well, my Monstrous Thing, there is but one thing thou should-" she's cut off as my entire body tenses in pain. I feel it immediately. The change. The bloom. Like my whole body is on fire. It hasn't happened so fast before. It hasn't hurt this much. It's like Teratranza chewing me up again. I wasn't awake for the other changes. I didn't think I could be awake for them, but I am, and I am in so much pain. It rips me out of my daze and quickly brings me to my hands and knees.

I can feel my bones in my legs breaking and reforming. Parts of my face split open as something pushes through the new holes. My vision blurs and crosses. I can't seem to focus on anything. I can feel the sides of my lips begin to tear and teeth begin to ache. The cuts in my palms from my claws expand and begin to shift on their own. I feel my sternum break in half and my ribs growing through my muscles. I'm aware of everything as my body shifts and changes.

This is it. This is penance for what I've done. For killing Alex. My horns ache, my tail aches, but most of all, my heart aches with their absence.

The process is as slow as eating Alex was and as painful as it must've been for Justin and Amanda.

I can't tell how much time has passed, but by the time the pain begins to subside my throat is raw from screaming.

"Thou art finally thyself," Teratranza says in awe. "My most beautiful child, my Monstrosity, how does it feel?" My breathing is ragged and I can barely recognize my voice as I respond, "I feel better than ever." I respond as I genuinely do. My body feels lighter, stronger, and stranger than ever. A pleasant buzz fills my body.

I no longer sound like me though. My voice now sounds like Alex. Their voice, Teratranza's, and mine are all layered together. My voice is its own eerie harmony, and it makes me miss the sound of Alex's voice on its own already.

"Damn! I look good on you!" Exclaims a familiar voice. No.

No it can't be. My brain's playing tricks on me. But I can't help but look up.

Floating there, in the air right before me, is Alex. Whole and unharmed. Their eyes glow an uncanny green.

I can't do anything but stare. They cross their arms, with the widest grin I've ever seen on their face, before asking, "What? You miss me already?"

Chapter 17

BLOOM

I try to leap towards Alex to embrace them, but find even standing difficult. My legs feel strange. I look back and see my legs with new joints and bent at a strange angle. Digitigrade, I think it's called. My pants are stretched to their limit and beginning to rip. My shoes are destroyed entirely by the new talons ripping through them. What used to be my feet are now somewhere between a wolf's paw and an eagle's talon, and all of it that same dark shade of red from my previous changes.

I look back to Alex. They're floating inches from my face and it takes me several seconds to be able to focus on their face. It's just the same as before. No changes. They're in the air at a fortyfive degree angle, head down towards me and feet way up high.

"How?" Is all I can manage as I reach out a hand towards them.

I pause as I notice something, a flash of white on my palm. Teeth. I turn my hand and see a jagged and miniature maw running across my hand. I look and see it's all my hands. My vision swims as I take everything in. My entire hands are also red up to a few inches past the wrist. I look back at Alex who, for their part, looks pleased with themselves.

"While I would in fact die for you, I couldn't let you mourn me. I may or may not have had a longshot plan. I was dead the second you finished swallowing me. Instantly gone. It was... strange. My soul ended up meeting your lovely demon." Alex explains as they see my bafflement.

"I was just about to absorb this Clever thing's soul, before they made me an offer." Chimes in Teratranza from the palm of one of my hands. That's definitely new.

"You can only make one deal at a time?" Is all I can think to ask. "I died. My deal was up!" Alex cheers. "So I struck a new deal."

"Their soul shall serve me forever more, my Monstrosity," answers the demon in turn, "and by extension, that includes my children."

I'm so dumbfounded that Alex begins to chuckle.

"You're stuck with me now, Dax!" Alex is grinning like an idiot, blood still trickling down the sides of their mouth like nothing's changed at all. It drips to the floor but disappears as it would land.

It's then that I focus on Alex further. As I gaze at them, I realize I can see the window behind them through their face. Alex is ever so faintly translucent. Except for their eyes, It's like looking through stained glass.

"You're... what? A ghost now then?" I ask still in shock. I want to reach out and pull them to me, but the idea that I'd pass right through them is too terrifying. To be forever haunted by them without the ability to touch them again would be a pain too deep for me to bear after our one and only kiss.

"Hmm," Alex contemplates for a second. "I suppose I am, but there's more details to the bargain we struck. I can still do this afterall."

Alex then floats upright, flush with me, and I feel their body against me. I feel as their hands cup my jaw, and most of all I feel when they kiss me again. It tastes of their sweetest blood, but I don't feel myself losing control of myself.

They feel so perfect against me. I wrap my arms around them and squeeze them tight as we share our second kiss. The fireworks have yet to go away by the time I pull my head back and I feel genuinely light headed.

"See? A ghost you can touch." Alex says in a hushed, sultry tone. A shiver runs up my spine and my tail starts to flick on its own. Alex lets out a small laugh as they see this. They then begin to study my face. "Yup, it's just as I thought. Your new mouth is just as fun to kiss."

"New mouth?" I ask in a momentary daze. Oh! I almost forgot in the joy that is Alex, that my body should finally be changed.

"I understand being lost in love, my Monstrosity. Now is also the time to become lost in love of thyself. Gaze upon thy new form and witness the utter beauty that is thy blooming!" Teratranza commands from every maw at once. Five voices layered over each other. I take a closer look at my hand as I remove one arm from Alex.

I can feel it. I can feel them all. I move them open and closed. This feels right. I feel right, right now, and yet so different at the same time. I look up to Alex who is simply gazing up at me with clear adoration. How could they have hidden this expression from me for so long? My stomach flutters at the sight.

155

"So this is you, huh?" Says Alex. "The real you? I like it. It suits you. You should take a look." We release each other and I try to stand but fumble. The pain effects of all that pain have yet to fully leave me. The ache of breaking bones and splitting skin still lives in very recent memory and echoes across my body when I move.

"Can you grab me the mirror?" I request from Alex. Their smile drops for a second.

"No can do. I can only touch you and other children of Teratranza. If there are any that is. Only you can see me too. I'm all yours." Their smile returns as they say that last sentence. They offer their hands to me and I reach out and accept their assistance with all four of mine.

I slowly make my way to my feet. My legs feel almost asleep. I stretch and flex them. My thighs are still stretching the fabric pleasantly. I didn't lose any of my more feminine features by the looks of it. My walking feels more like stalking with my new legs.

I prowl towards the mirror as I hunch slightly. I'm taller than before. Easily seven feet tall now and then some.

It's only then that I notice my hair. I can see it when I look down. It's past my shoulders now. Long black hair like Alex's. A wavy mess tangled mess unlike their straight hair but I know this is from them. A piece of them shining through me. I smile ear to ear. Literally, as I feel my lips curl upwards. I frown then, confused. Just how much has changed? What do I look like now?

I reach the mirror and what I see in it is simply stunning.

My new and improved face has suddenly grown several more eyes. Five more by the looks of it. All sharp and yellow, four in a line with my original eyes, one above and one below each, and one on my forehead completely vertical. The eyes seem to form an arching shape. Most of a circle. They're all looking slightly different directions. Every single one of them is surrounded by a tinge of red.

My horns are much larger now. Spiraling further back and pointing farther forward. They're clearly in my vision now as I start to focus all my eyes together. My hair cascades behind me, most of it still tied together at the end with a ribbon. The rest of it sticking out this way and that like a rats nest.

My mouth extends its previous length to either side, tripling its size. I bare my teeth and my sharp fangs extend that far back as well. I open my mouth and it opens much more and far wider than before. The joint of my jaw feels further back. I smile and it looks absolutely disturbing. I look perfect.

Finally, I notice my abdomen. The Maw is still there, but it's distinctly different. While it still extends horizontally across my stomach, there seems to be a second set of teeth going down vertically from somewhere under my crop top. It appears to start at my pant line and goes up, through and past the original Maw all the way up to my collar bone as I raise my ragged shirt.

I hear a whistle from behind me from Alex as I do so. I laugh and blush just a little, but I focus on the Maws.

The corners where this upside down cross shape meet are pointed diagonally towards the center. The two interlocking Maws' teeth are seamless and continuous next to each other.

I try to open my Maw by leaning backwards like before. It works. The other set stays closed. I then close it and focus on the new vertical set of teeth. Where my sternum split and ribs grew into deadly fangs. I rip myself apart as my vertical mouth opens up to reveal the same void and tongue. Back and towards the center of my seemingly hollow abdomen. It feels strange and alien but not bad at all. I finally splay myself as I open both Maws at once and my whole body opens up. It's horrific and terrible as my entire body turns into one massive, gaping Maw. It's a display of sheer freakishness, but it feels like me. This all feels like me.

As I close my new and improved Maws, I find myself tearing up, almost overwhelmed by everything. Alex hugs me from behind, apparently having floated up to me.

"How do you feel?" They ask me, muffled into my back. I raise my arms to hold their arms in place. I lift my tail to gently wrap around them in an attempt to hug them back. To keep them close to me like this.

"I feel free. I feel like myself. I feel... happy." I answer, choking up. Alex squeezes me tighter.

"I'm happy too." Alex murmurs. "Hey Alex?" I begin, a little nervous. "Yeah?" They answer back.

"I've been thinking about names," I say, mustering up the strength to do this. "I want to leave Daxton behind with my old self."

"Oh! I've been waiting for this moment! What have you got?" Alex declares excitedly. I can't help but smile. Of course they were looking forward to this. Alex had me clocked before I ever told them.

"Don't judge me too harshly, but I was thinking about Scylla. You know from the Odyssey? The woman turned into a monster and all. It can mean 'She Who Rends'. Felt fitting."

"'For Scylla is not mortal; Moreover she is savage, extreme, rude, cruel and invincible'," Alex replies. "That sounds about right for you. I love it!"

"Did you just quote the Odyssey to me?" I ask incredulously. "Maybe." Alex answers with obvious delight.

"Save the dirty talk for later." I request jokingly.

"Yes, thou may continue later. Thou may now thank me at any time thou wishes." Teratranza teases as her voice echoes through the different maws on my hands.

"Thank you, Teratranza." I say smiling, with all the sincerity I feel. Without her, none of this would have been possible. I would have stayed the same old me and Alex would have left me all alone eventually. Now I can look at my muscled, hulking, curvy, monstrous self and be genuinely happy with what I see. I can hold Alex close to me once again.

"Thou art welcome. Alas, I shall take my leave. But know this! Thou must simply call upon my name, and I will answer, oh Monstrous child. I am still here for thee." She says with the care she held in her voice the first time she called me beautiful. I feel that way now. I am beautiful. I always have been.

"Goodbye then. I'll make sure to call." I say with warmth. "Good." Is the last thing she says.

Alex and I stand there for a good while longer. For a ghost, they're still so warm. It's Alex who speaks first yet again.

"Well, Scylla, I believe it was you who asked 'what happens now?'. My turn to ask a question. I'm asking you the same thing." Says Alex after I let them go and they float up next to me, nudging my side with their head like a cat.

I genuinely hadn't thought about it. I didn't think I'd make it this far alive. I didn't think Alex and I could ever be together. I didn't think I'd actually achieve my dreams of transformation. I didn't think I could ever be this happy. I always thought I'd die trying and fighting for everything that mattered to me.

I fish out of my pocket the somehow intact photo of Alex and I from their birthday. We both look at it and grin. I walk over to the next room and set it down on the table next to the gun and flashlight.

"Now? We start to live as ourselves. As we finally are. Together." I reply with confidence I don't feel but hope present in my voice.

"I'd like that." Alex says simply. They float up and plant a kiss on my cheek. "Let's see what a Monster and Ghost can do." A wicked grin crosses their face.

We leave the cabin together, and disappear into the surrounding woods.

EPILOGUE

"In the weeks that followed the sudden disappearance of four high schoolers under strange circumstances, police temporarily shut down the school. Teachers and parents alike were questioned about the large mysterious pool of blood found in the bowels of the school and any strange behaviors the students may have been exhibiting.

Accounts of the missing students' behaviors revealed little beyond a minor argument between one of the missing students, Daxton Meyers, and a teacher, Regina Slade, before Daxton's disappearance.

Investigations into the parents and teachers grinded to a halt when the body of Phil Meyers, Daxton's father, was discovered butchered and mutilated in his own home. Daxton's mother, Doreen Meyers was only able to properly identify the body via a watch that Phil always wore, his face and other identifiable features a brutal mess. Further investigations into the home revealed the door to Daxton's room being broken down, and his room in absolute disarray, with bed, clothes and even walls appearing to be shredded by something sharp.

Following these gruesome scenes, a trail of bodies began to litter the town. Doreen Meyers was the next to be found, outside a local bar, in the alley the next morning. Her body showed evidence of multiple broken bones and deep laceration covered what remained of her body. Following this, the parents of another one of the missing students, Alexander Hernandez, were both found dead in a car crash, their car wrapped around a tree. Eileen and Roger Hernandez had, however, been ripped apart in a manner befitting a large animal by the time they were discovered. The final body to be found belonged to that of the teacher, Regina Slade. Her remains were clearly dumped on the doors of the school in the middle of the night. The school's cameras reportedly caught nothing but an indistinct blur before the body mysteriously appeared. Her home showed no signs of forced entry.

Every single one of these bodies showed evidence of both bite and claw marks, inconsistent with any local animals.

Searches for the missing students continued, spurred on by the hopeful parents of Amanda and Justin Foster. While primary suspects in the investigation, Christina and George Foster cooperated with authorities and no evidence against them was ever found.

Investigations for the missing students took to the woods, which revealed only stranger circumstances still. The carcasses of deers, coyotes, and bears had all been found to litter the woods throughout and surrounding the town.

Strange voices and laughter reportedly echoed through the woods at night and the woods quickly became synonymous with danger and strange happenings to the residents of the town. The source of the disappearances, deaths, and mutilations were never found. Investigators called the case unsolvable despite the scale of the events.

Rumors and fear quickly spread amongst the town's residents as events transpired and the entity behind it all quickly gained many names and stories. Every pet that went missing for a day or bump in the night was blamed on the very same entity.

Some have even claimed to see the creature, and though few among them could agree on its features beyond resembling a larger than life woman, these individuals all agreed on the fear it instilled in them. Reports of these sightings had to be gathered mostly from people who had left the town shortly after seeing the creature, as if their encounters had shaken them badly enough to flee.

Known by the names 'The Butcher Beast', 'The Voices of Violence', and 'The Massacre Woman', this mysterious and brutal creature is known primarily for one thing: Its ravenous hunger."

— An excerpt from "Cold Cases, Cryptids, and Curses". An informative, if dramatic, blog into mysterious and supernatural events.